THE HARLEQUIN PROTOCOL

PREQUEL TO THE ELIOUD LEGACY SERIES

LIANE ZANE

ZEPHON ROMANCE
BOSTON, MASSACHUSETTS

Digital Edition JANUARY 2024 ISBN: 978-1-963515-01-5

Print Edition ISBN: 978-1-963515-02-2

Audiobook Edition ISBN: 978-1-963515-03-9

Cover design by Betelgeuse, 99Designs

To L.M. and A.S.

The struggle is real. Thank you both for having my back as we fight the good fight.

ONE

Olivia Markham loved the Advent season in Germany. There was nothing quite like the outdoor markets that abounded throughout the country in the weeks leading up to Christmas, where artisans and craftspeople displayed handcrafted wares such as jewelry and wooden toys. The Christmas Market at the Kaiser Wilhelm Memorial Church in Breitscheidplatz in Berlin, one of the city's largest, featured a Ferris wheel and carousel along with daily visits from Santa, who distributed gifts to children.

As Olivia and her partner, Thomas, wended through the throngs, she sniffed the air, filled with sharp longing for a moment. It was the first time she wouldn't be home for Christmas.

On the plaza around them, warm scents of caramelized almonds and *lebkuchen*—the lightly spiced German version of gingerbread—mixed in a hunger-inducing dance with roasted pork, sausages, and chestnuts. Happy people, tourists and locals alike, wandered through nearly 200 quaint stalls that harkened back to the

Middle Ages, drinking mulled *glühwein* while munching on cake-like glazed *stollen* stuffed with dried fruits and nuts.

Too bad Olivia couldn't enjoy it as an ordinary visitor.

Instead, she gripped Thomas's hand and sipped the hot chocolate she held in the other—a convenient prop—and consigned the tantalizing scents to a background blur along with the Christmas lights and chatter. Surveillance work, though vital in pinpointing extremist threats, often meant long, tedious hours in discomfort and boredom. At least today they got to walk outside. They'd spent the last three weeks inside a cramped flat listening to phone calls for Moroccan takeout and reviewing hours of photos and videos.

The dark-haired man that she and Thomas followed had entered the market from Kurfürstendamm, the three-and-a-half kilometer shopping boulevard that formed the heartline of the western city center. On the other side of the traditional Christmas market, the boulevard changed names and led to the Europa Center mall. If they didn't lose him among the mass of shoppers outside, they'd struggle to keep sight of him if he entered the building.

Late last year, the target had come onto the radar of German Federal Intelligence, the *Bundesnachrichtendienst* or BND as it was known in the intelligence community, after a trip to Afghanistan. The BND had alerted its American counterpart when it discovered evidence that Hafid Alami had visited Bagram Air Force base. Now the two intelligence agencies shared a joint operation on what had all the hallmarks of a terrorist cell in Berlin. Today's surveillance fell on the CIA team, which included Olivia and Thomas.

Alami slowed and began studying the stalls nearest him. Olivia and Thomas drifted closer to a small marionette theater where a gigantic wooden Nutcracker and toy soldiers battled a bevy of mice led by the Mouse King. Tchaikovsky's famous ballet music played in tinny exhilaration from speakers embedded in the wooden stage.

Across from them, Olivia saw a group of immigrant men surrounding several women near a 15-meter wooden Christmas pyramid topped by an iconic large propeller. From the angry looks on the women's faces and the sharp sounds of rapid German, she suspected that the men harassed them. It was becoming more and more a problem as immigrants from the Middle East and Africa, escaping the increasing turmoil of the 'Arab Spring,' made their way to the more peaceful—and prosperous—Western Europe, especially Germany, where Chancellor Merkel's policies sought to bolster their integration.

Olivia dragged her gaze away. It wasn't in her mission brief to mediate social tensions. She had to stay focused on their objective. They needed more information on Alami, his local connections, and where he went outside of his Berlin flat. They needed to know who ran him.

None of the known terrorist organizations had any chatter about Alami, yet the young Moroccan had traveled four times to the Mideast in the past two years. And, despite the care he took to mask his movements, his regular visits to hawaladar brokers suggested foreign communications. In the past two weeks, Alami had traveled outside of Berlin several times, once as far as Belgium.

Something was coming.

It was possible that Alami ran a self-contained cell with three or four members, but Thomas suspected a local handler gave this foot soldier his orders. A handler deeply connected with al-Qaeda and the power vacuum from Bin Laden's death. Olivia had dubbed this shadowy leader 'Mr. X' in her head. Thomas had ordered today's full-court surveillance press out of sheer frustration at their lack of leads. He'd already decided that they should subvert the joint operation and snatch Alami if the opportunity presented itself.

Thomas glanced at her. "We should split up. We're about to go hot." He trained his gaze on their subject again. "Alami seems to have an uncanny ability to move among crowds. He's likely got enough training to run an SDR."

Surveillance Detection Route was the term of art used by the CIA to describe the protocol field officers used to flush out foreign agents watching them. Thomas had been a CIA officer long enough that he'd developed an almost-preternatural sense of when their target used the tactic against *them*.

Right on cue, Alami entered a large stall selling flame-seared meats. The Moroccan had just created a chokepoint: Olivia and Thomas couldn't follow him into the stall. Either they kept walking or they pretended to shop where they were. Loitering near the stall where the target now ordered food was out of the question.

Olivia nodded. "I'll tag Jade Doll as the new eyeball."

The 'eyeball' was whoever on the team followed the target—a key component in defeating an SDR because it made it harder for the target to identify a tail.

What if Alami has cell members watching his route? asked a small inner voice as Olivia peered at the spectators, mostly young families.

Her gaze strayed to the immigrants, who'd clustered on the far side of the plaza, a dark, surly knot in a cheerful sea of shoppers. But there was no time to ponder the possibility of other cell members at the Christmas market. They had to stay focused despite all of the noise.

Olivia activated her bone mic. "Jade, you're up."

Monica, her teammate from her early CIA training days, responded. "Copy that."

Olivia and Thomas separated, he to approach a stall offering traditional German fare of beer and brats, she to go closer to one selling handblown glass ornaments that sparkled under warm white lights. Even though the angle of her view prevented Olivia from fully seeing inside the stall where the Moroccan now stood at a counter waiting for his food, she'd know if he left. She could also keep watch over anyone entering or leaving.

Monica leapfrogged their location, moving beyond Alami to take up position in front of a kiosk selling Nutcracker soldiers.

"Eyes on," she said to their team via comm.

Olivia relaxed a little, letting herself scan the busy promenade between the highly decorated stalls. Groups of shoppers sat on round stone benches, while others loitered around the numerous Christmas trees or meandered from counter to counter. No one was in a hurry to go home on this mild November evening.

The marionette performance ended. Families gathered children and began to stream away in little clumps, tugging on reluctant hands and pushing strollers laden with toddlers and purchases. The blue of the sky had deepened against the bright kiosk lights. Above the plaza, the bombed shell of the original Kaiser Wilhem Memorial Church loomed. Nicknamed 'The Hollow Tooth," the Neo-Romanesque ruins projected a grim reminder of humanity's capacity for evil.

A large male on the far side of the plaza caught Olivia's attention. Something in the way that he moved reminded her of *Sensei* Mark, her college karate coach.

He glanced over his shoulder, his vivid blue gaze honing in on hers. A shiver moved down her spine. She took an involuntary step forward.

The crowd shifted, and the male disappeared behind a trio of bearded men who reminded her of the other group of immigrants, though she didn't recognize any of them. Their deeper voices, previously masked in the general noise and chatter, reached her ears through some trick of the ebb and flow of sound. The immigrants spoke an unfamiliar Maghrebi dialect, the form of Arabic spoken in northwestern Africa, but Olivia caught the gist of their derogatory comments, saw their hostile glances toward a group of oblivious young women, who laughed as they drank wine and shopped for Christmas presents.

Olivia frowned.

Then the vendor selling the handblown glass ornaments came closer, smiling and asking if she could help Olivia with anything.

Get your head in the game, Olivia reminded herself.

Smiling back at the woman, Olivia gestured toward a teardrop-shaped ornament featuring an angel dressed in a blue gown. As she did, the painted blonde's gaze snagged her attention. It almost looked as if the ethereal figure actually recognized her.

Olivia blinked and asked the vendor to wrap the ornament for purchase before glancing towards the target.

Alami, now visible, stood outside the seared-meat stall at a wooden bar, scrolling through his cellphone screen as if he didn't have a care in the world.

Olivia narrowed her eyes. What was Alami doing in a German Christmas market?

"A lone male approaches this stall. He's got line of sight with the target," said Thomas over the comm.

Olivia handed the German shopkeeper some cash, telling her to keep the change, and accepted the bagged Christmas ornament. As she turned away, her sight returned almost against her volition to the three obnoxious immigrants, who'd taken on a menacing penumbra—as if their dark intents clouded the air around them. They'd surrounded a young woman, blocking her exit into the flow of pedestrians. Something in the way that she held herself, her eyes wide, told Olivia in an instant that terror gripped the woman.

She shot a look at Thomas, who'd ordered a stein of beer and tilted the frosty plastic mug to his mouth, his own gaze casually sweeping the crowd. Monica, now holding a nutcracker and working the lever of its lower jaw, laughed at the shopkeeper who stood next to her. Though she appeared engrossed in trying out the handmade traditional toy, Olivia saw Monica's gaze repeatedly focus on Alami over the shopkeeper's shoulder.

"Wind Walker?" asked Olivia into her bone mic. She slipped the bagged ornament into a large shopping bag carried by an oblivious middle-aged woman.

Bryce, the final member of their team, answered. "Go for Wind Walker."

"You hanging around?" Olivia maneuvered closer to the trio, who'd shifted twenty meters back toward Kurfürstendamm. The young woman was nowhere to be seen.

"I'm in position."

Olivia knew that the tall Texan, who moved like a panther despite his size, would be a silent shadow on Monica's six, coming no closer than ten meters unless necessary.

Not too far to help Thomas or Monica if something should happen either with Alami, who'd just returned to the seared-meats stall for a tray of food, or the new male that Thomas had identified. And, really the plaza wasn't that big. She could be back within moments, if the team needed her.

Where was the young woman? Olivia's gaze raked the throng around the area where the trio had been standing, widening her survey in ever-increasing arcs. Although the crowd was polite, shifting as shoppers moved among stalls, the woman couldn't have gotten far in the few minutes that Olivia's vision had been off of her. Her bright blond hair had been a beacon.

One member of the trio had disappeared as well.

Tossing her hot chocolate into the nearest trash bin, Olivia swore and used her elbows to get through the people around her. Shoppers threw startled glances and sharp words at her but let her pass. She blended and merged, swimming through narrow open channels between people as she'd learned to do over the past two years in fieldwork.

Now the crowd absorbed the other two members of the trio.

"Sweet Pea, where're you going?" came Thomas's irritated voice in Olivia's ear.

Olivia didn't have time to explain. Her neck tingled, and her St. Michael medal burned. "Right back, Sundance," she said instead.

The comm hissed as Thomas swore.

Olivia rushed toward the tall male blocking the corner of the stall where she'd last seen the trio of immigrants. He had a head and shoulders on her and weighed at least thirty kilos more than she did, but Olivia's training had taught her how to leverage physical inflection points. As the male flinched away from her, Olivia stepped into his side, forcing his balance to shift farther. Crying out, he stumbled into the wooden structure.

She ignored him. Her internal alarm shrieked at her, her pulse ratcheting up even though she had barely covered any distance since leaving her position. Another, rational, voice murmured orders to return to her team and its mission. She ignored it as well.

A man wearing a stained white apron under a puffy dark winter jacket and holding a large white bucket stood in the narrow alley ahead of her. Just beyond him was the old church's Tuff-stone façade. Suddenly, Olivia knew where the young woman and the trio of men had gone: the memorial hall in the base of the damaged spire.

She sprinted forward. The cook, or whoever he was, managed to step out of her way.

The ringing of the carillon bells at the top of the hour swallowed the sounds of the plaza behind her, increasing Olivia's sense of urgency. She pulled her Sig from its hidden shoulder holster, holding it in both hands with the muzzle pointed up as she ran.

Olivia rounded the end of the stall where it formed another alley with the medieval-looking tower. She threw out a hand, catching herself on the rough volcanic rock as she changed direction, running toward the boulevard and the front of the old church. Her breathing remained easy, and her light steps scarcely registered on the pavement.

She rushed around the corner to the entrance door, tugging it just wide enough to slip inside. She halted.

There were more than three men. The blonde's bright hair gleamed among the shifting legs around her. Voices rode one over another, rough laughter and excitement bouncing off the walls. No one noticed Olivia.

Her heart lunged to her throat.

In the next thirty seconds, everything changed on the plaza outside.

"Backpack!" Thomas's terse voice punched the comm channel. "He's headed your way, Wind Walker."

"I'm on him," said Bryce.

"Jade?"

"Target hasn't moved. He hasn't even looked up from his phone."

"Don't let him out of your sight. I've got the backpack."

"Sweet Pea, where are you?" Cold anger threaded Thomas's voice.

Olivia didn't answer. She didn't think she could.

Then he broke the spell. "Backpack wired with explosives. *Get him,* Wind Walker."

Olivia's heart stuttered several beats. *Thomas. IED.*

For a moment, she was paralyzed. The image of Thomas leaning over her, an intent look in his dark eyes, flashed across her mind's eye.

"Second target's entered the mall." Bryce's cool voice belied the new danger.

If the second target wore a bomb vest under his winter coat....

"I'm on my way," she said, the bone mic vibrating against her jaw.

Before Olivia could react, the sea of legs parted, and the blonde's wide gaze above a restraining hand caught hers. The hand on her mouth belonged to the man raping her.

Olivia lowered the Sig and shot several of the attackers, including the man on top of the blonde. Grunts and cries filled the hall. Most of the attackers scattered, taking refuge behind the marble columns along the walls, though two turned and charged Olivia.

A resounding *boom* shook the old tower, threatening to bring down the last of the structure that the Allied bombers hadn't in 1943.

The rushing attackers hesitated for a moment.

Bad mistake, thought Olivia, no longer paralyzed.

She shot each once, center-mass. One fell to the side, his mouth open and an arm bent protectively over his chest. A gurgling sound came from his mouth as he lay stunned and blinking. The other man lurched a few steps forward before falling on his knees in front of her.

Olivia narrowed her eyes as she looked down on him.

"Enjoy Paradise," she said in Darija, the "everyday" Moroccan dialect of Maghrebi Arabic she was sure he spoke.

Then she pushed him out of her way with her hip. He thudded to the floor.

When she reached the victim, the woman managed to rise from the floor into a sitting position, one arm propping her upright. Her bright hair tangled in a cloud around her head. Her pants and underwear had been pulled to her calves, and blood welled on her stomach. Beneath her an incongruous mosaic of a winged and robed saint speared a man-headed beast through his open throat.

Olivia stood over the woman, looking around at the remaining men. "Flee, cowards, before I empty my gun in you," she said in Darija. If there was any justice, they would feel more exposed and less willing to act knowing that someone understood their speech. "There will be no place in Paradise for you then."

The men fled, the wounded helped by their uninjured friends and trailing blood.

Olivia held her hand out to the woman, anxious to return to the plaza and her team. What would she find? There had been nothing from any of them since the explosion....

"Come," she said in German.

The woman grabbed her hand, the glazed look on her face confirming that she acted on autopilot, and stood. Olivia bent to pull the woman's pants and underwear up. That's when she saw that the attackers had used a sharp blade to cut through the waistband of the victim's pants and underwear, and that they had sliced the skin of her stomach with its tip in their haste.

Or perhaps deliberately.

"Bastards," said Olivia in English, glancing over her shoulder at the two dead men. She wanted to kill the rest of them.

The woman startled at her speech. Olivia apologized in soft German, modulating her voice to a soothing tone. She made to drop the victim's hand, but the woman clutched hers as if drowning. Olivia assured her that she wasn't letting go. She tucked her Sig into its holster and managed to get her own belt off one-handed before threading it through the belt loops on the victim's pants.

The whole time, seconds ticked off Olivia's internal clock. Some part of her screamed inside a soundproof room in her head, pounding and pounding to be let out, to run out on the plaza yelling for Thomas.

Instead, she cinched her belt tight, pulling the severed halves of the woman's waistband closed. The victim cried out, once, and Olivia winced, but she finished threading the belt's tip through the buckle and secured it before standing upright.

"What's your name?" she asked, carefully adjusting the woman's sweater as she did to hide the blood seeping through the front of her pants. When the woman didn't respond, Olivia tried again, this time looking into the woman's eyes. She swallowed rising impatience.

The woman, blinking as if clearing dust from her eyes, focused on Olivia. "Anja."

"Anja, my name's Olivia. I'm going to take you back to the Christmas Market and find someone to take you to the hospital."

Anja blinked some more as if she was translating Olivia's words into a language she didn't speak well. Her gazed strayed to the bodies on the floor beyond them. Olivia's breath sucked in before she could stop it, but then she held it, counting to ten as she let it out. No need to sigh like a diva when Anja's world had just shifted on its axis.

"All right," said Anja, looking back at Olivia.

Olivia led Anja by the hand outside the old church. The distinctive chemical smell of explosives wafted through the air. Above the babble of voices and the noise of traffic, the clear sound of sirens wailed. They had to wend their way through people milling around as more poured from the entrance of the Christmas market, wandering in a daze.

Olivia scanned the plaza next to the boulevard. It took several seconds before she identified the site of the blast.

The carnival ride about twenty meters into the plaza tilted dangerously on its side, its black bulk ominous among the Christmas lights adorning the surrounding wooden stalls. An image of the open panel to the mechanics flashed into Olivia's memory. She'd noted that the ride hadn't been running when they'd first entered the Christmas market. Thomas must have as well.

Please, God, she thought, unable to form more words in the mute prayer.

Olivia pushed against the flow of people into the market, scarcely aware that Anja followed, clinging to her hand with both of hers. As they approached the metal husk, Olivia felt jagged pieces of metal under her feet. Anja stumbled and would have fallen if Olivia hadn't managed to catch her. That's when Olivia saw one of the ride's cars, a flying boat, on its side, wedged into the front of a stall selling freshly baked *lebkuchen*. And then she saw more car-size shrapnel in a ten-meter blast radius.

Olivia and Anja stopped.

Olivia had no idea how long they'd been standing there, silent before this memorial to hatred, when she heard Thomas's hoarse voice behind them.

"There you are. Where the hell did you disappear to?"

Olivia turned, Anja's hand still gripping hers. Her heart raced in complex emotion: relief, joy, trepidation. Thomas's dark eyes glinted in the plaza lights.

"And why did you burn this mission?"

Two

Twelve hours later, Olivia sat in a windowless conference room at the BND headquarters waiting for her doom to arrive. She hadn't been back to the flat she shared with Monica since the attack, and she could smell herself, the scent of rank sweat mixed with coppery blood that clung to her clothes, skin, and hair. Half-finished cold coffee in a white porcelain cup sat on the table where she'd pushed it away from her. She had no idea how Anja fared or where the rest of her team was being debriefed.

Olivia sighed and shoved a hand through her tangled hair. She didn't even have her bag with mints and ibuprofen. The BND had taken her weapon and her purse when she arrived. American intelligence officers got a lot of leeway when working with friendly countries, especially when it came to terrorism, but that didn't mean that she didn't have a lot to answer for.

She looked down at her left hand where the gold wedding band and modest diamond engagement ring glinted in the bright overhead lights. Pulling her hand closer, she ran her thumb against the bands.

It wasn't what she'd dreamed of as a teenager mooning over her first boyfriend. Nor was it what she'd secretly hoped would happen between her and Thomas.

Then again, why would she have imagined having to file a "close-and-continuing" notice with the CIA human resources department when she finally dated someone? Or that she'd then have to pretend to be his wife for a mission?

Her left hand strayed to the St. Michael medal on her chest. She missed *Sensei* Mark and his karate classes. True, she'd gotten some very tough training at The Farm, and Sam's camps with special forces and the Special Activities Division had honed her skills in a way that her college martial arts team couldn't. But she couldn't shake the feeling that *Sensei* Mark really cared about *her*, that he wasn't just training one of dozens of operatives for the U.S.

The door behind Olivia opened with a sharp *click*. A tall, spare man with high cheekbones and thin light-brown hair strode in carrying a manila file folder.

He came around the other side of the table but didn't sit.

"Ms. Markham," he said in English with a German accent, one palm running along the edge of the folder as he studied her.

So. A BND interrogator.

Olivia dipped her chin and held his gaze. "Where is my team?" she asked in German, not bothering to pretend that she was a tourist.

The folder was likely the BND file on her, which was essentially an abbreviated version of her personnel file. By now the BND had added its own notes from the joint operation *and* the Christmas Market bombing.

The German intelligence officer took a moment to answer, his gaze shrewd and assessing. "Still filling in details of the attack on the Christmas market." He continued to speak in English.

"I should be with them," she said, still answering in German. What was this man's game?

"You should have been with them on the Breitscheidplatz, Ms. Markham."

Olivia resisted squirming under his sharp stare. Instead, she answered honestly. "Yes, I should have."

"Why did you follow the men who attacked Fraulein Müller?"

Olivia's temper flared. "'Attacked'? What the hell is wrong with you, *Klaus*?" Olivia didn't know the man's name but wanted to needle him. Her St. Michael medal, like her temper, heated under her fingertips. She realized she was holding it and dropped it to stare at the German intelligence officer. "She was raped, for Godsake!"

He ignored her gibe. "Did you know that the two men you killed are recent refugees of the Syrian Civil War?"

"By way of the Maghreb?" asked Olivia, her tone mocking.

Now the BND interrogator responded. His eyes narrowed. Leaning forward, he said, "Ms. Markham, I don't think you know how much trouble you're in." This time he said it in German.

Olivia's heart beat faster, but she shrugged. Then she leaned forward and held his gaze without blinking.

"Not really worried about me, Klaus. I want to learn about Anja, the casualties, and my team. It doesn't matter in what order." She spoke in German using the tone of voice that Sam Ahren, her former handler, had used with the spec-ops soldiers he trained for the Company.

The other intelligence officer's eyes widened. Pulling out the chair across from Olivia, he sat and said nothing for a moment.

Then he said, "My name's Dieter." He paused. "Dieter Klaus. How did you know my last name?"

Olivia shrugged again, but an eerie sense flitted through her. She had no idea how that name had popped in her head. She'd just gone with it. But it seemed to have rattled the German interrogator.

"It's not really about either of us. Did you know that the men in the church included immigrants from North Africa?"

Dieter shook his head, watching her. "How do you know that?"

"I heard some of them speaking in Maghrebi Arabic. It was definitely a Moroccan dialect. I caught some Berber words."

"Is that why you followed them?"

"Not entirely," said Olivia, her right hand going for the coffee cup and spinning it.

She knew that it telegraphed unwanted information to this shrewd interrogator, who was likely cataloguing everything she said and looking for a thread with which to unravel her. But her nerves had tightened unbearably. She had to get out of here before she choked this man out with his own tie and went on a search mission for her team.

"Are you suggesting that your gut, as you Americans say, led you to the church?" Now Dieter sounded skeptical.

Olivia brought her hard stare back to his face. "I followed a trio of men speaking Darija who'd been harassing Anja on the plaza moments before. My *gut* told me that they planned to make good their threats to her."

Scenting blood, her interlocuter leaned forward. "Your defense of Ms. Müller had nothing to do with the surveillance of Hafid Alami, the subject of a joint mission between our countries?"

It wasn't really a question.

"I wouldn't say nothing," said Olivia, pulling her fingers from the cup and sitting back. "The timing of the rape is too great a coincidence. One of the men on the plaza did most of the speaking. It's true he used a different Maghrebi dialect than Alami, but he also disappeared. He wasn't in the old church with the others."

Dieter considered her words. "Let's say the two incidents are related. What was the purpose of the assault?"

"A distraction." As soon as Olivia said this, she knew it was true. She sat forward, holding Dieter's gaze. "It wasn't supposed to happen in the church. It was supposed to happen on the plaza."

The BND officer didn't buy her explanation. "And you know this how?"

She shrugged. "My gut, as you said earlier."

Just then the door to the room opened, and Thomas came in, his face like a thundercloud and lightning in his gaze.

"Why is my operative still here?" he asked Dieter without looking at Olivia. "The rest of my team has finished their debrief. Alami and the bomber are in the wind. We need all our resources—and that includes Markham—to search for them."

Dieter opened the folder and shoved it across the table. Photos of the dead Syrian refugees inside the memorial hall greeted Olivia.

"This woman shot and killed two men in my country, Mr. Kincaid. Either she acted on your orders or she didn't. Either those men were associated with Hafid Alami or the bomber, or they weren't. Either she's a vigilante or you're holding out on us." He paused, his gaze hardening. "Which is it?"

"Neither," said Thomas, ignoring the photos and folding his arms across his chest. "Markham had operational flexibility to do whatever was necessary. I trust those under my command."

The implication that Dieter—and the BND as a whole—didn't do likewise with German officers or their American colleagues hung in the air around them.

"Now let my operative go. We've got bigger issues to deal with than whether Markham should have waited to fill out all of the paperwork to do the job your police force isn't."

Dieter's lips thinned. He pulled the folder back and stood. "Have it your way, Mr. Kincaid. But just remember that you and your team are here as a courtesy. Our willingness to share our intelligence extends only so far."

Thomas said nothing to Olivia until they were well away from the BND headquarters. Nevertheless, Olivia felt the tension in Thomas's posture, saw the tightness around his eyes.

"What the hell were you thinking?" he asked at last, turning his laser-sharp gaze on her. "That bomb could've killed a lot of people."

"But it didn't. More importantly, my being there wouldn't have made a lot of difference, would it?" asked Olivia, stung by the cold anger radiating from Thomas.

"Alami wouldn't have gotten away."

Olivia bristled. "You don't know that." Somewhere in the back of her mind she knew that she was retreating into anger as a defense. "I wasn't thinking, that's true. But some of those men spoke Darija."

Thomas's mien changed as a thoughtful expression replaced the hard one. He slowed his rapid strides. "That can't be a coincidence."

Olivia, who'd struggled to keep up, refrained from letting out a conspicuous sigh. "Thomas, you know I think you're right about Alami having a handler. What if he had something to do with immigrants raping the woman I rescued?"

"Shit." Thomas ran his fingers through his dark hair, making it wild. Olivia had the insanely irrelevant desire to smooth the strands.

He stopped and looked at her. "It doesn't matter. What's done is done, and we have no way of knowing if a handler—if he exists—orchestrated the bombing on the Breitscheidplatz. We have to focus on finding Alami before the Germans do. After your little stunt, by the time we're allowed to interrogate him, any intel he has will be staler than Bryce's gym socks."

Three hours later, after a nap, shower, and hot food, Olivia was at the field tactical operations center with the rest of the team. Bryce had given her a swift, one-armed hug when Thomas wasn't looking, while Monica handed her a travel mug of American-style coffee with a nod. She and Monica had a lot of experience together, and Olivia knew the other operative understood why Olivia had been compelled to rescue Anja.

Thomas stood with his arms crossed at the front of the small living area in the flat they'd filled with networked workstations. He dipped his chin at Olivia before calling their briefing to begin.

"Sitrep," he said to Monica.

And like that Olivia plunged back into the mission, which had gone hot. Their entire focus shifted now from observation to capture.

Monica, who'd been seeing a BND officer during their surveillance mission, brought the team up to speed on the intel her lover had shared with her, albeit unknowingly. Olivia didn't allow her ambivalence about this tactic to keep her from seeing the practical benefits. German intelligence slow-walked sharing information, it seemed. By the time the BND told Thomas that Alami had been spotted on CCTV in the western suburbs of Berlin, the team had already created a timeline of known sightings after the bombing.

Which was critical. Fifteen hours had already passed since the bomb exploded at the Christmas market. The longer they took to track Alami's whereabouts, the more likely he'd escape the intelligence net. And everyone's instincts, American and German alike, told them that it was only a matter of time before Alami tried again.

One key detail was confirmed, however: the backpack bomber and Alami traveled together. That they belonged in the same cell made operational sense, but it had only been conjecture by the American and German intelligence teams to this point.

"Okay, Monica," said Thomas after they reviewed the timeline, "go through our surveillance and match the sightings with locations for known contacts. For Alami to avoid capture this long, someone's got to be helping him. Bryce, dig into the backpack bomber. See if you can find something that the BND hasn't. Like a name."

Monica and Bryce nodded.

Thomas turned to Olivia. "We're going to go talk to Raif. He may have some idea who's financing Alami's getaway."

Olivia waited until Monica and Bryce had settled into their tasks before speaking to Thomas. "You don't need me to visit your pet hawaladar broker. In fact, he'd probably prefer you didn't bring an armed female to his place of business, visas or no visas."

She referred to the expedited U.S. visas that Thomas had arranged for the asset's parents to secure his loyalty. Olivia thought it was a pretty flimsy security.

Thomas, who'd been checking his messages on his phone, looked up at her. "Spit it out, Olivia. What do you want to do instead?"

"Interview the rape survivor. Maybe she saw something that can help us."

Thomas narrowed his eyes. "That sounds like a monumental waste of time. Doubtful that she understands Darija, let alone recalls details about any of the bastards who raped her."

Olivia didn't back down. "That sounds like you're prejudging the outcome. We're on a deadline, it's true. But can we really afford to overlook a possible eyewitness? One who may give us a lead on the larger network?"

He sighed harshly. "Go ahead. It's a waste of my time to argue with you. But Olivia? We're going to revisit the topic of your gut when things settle down a little. Understood?"

"Understood." Even as she said this, sharp hurt pierced Olivia before she stifled it.

Now wasn't the time for them. It was one of the drawbacks of dating the team leader.

Half an hour later, Olivia sat in Anja Müller's hospital room, enforced calm tamping the anger that had replaced her earlier hurt. She hadn't expected her job as an intelligence operative to require such emotional discipline, but this mission had tested her limits.

Anja hadn't looked at her yet. Instead, her fingers smoothed the sheet over her chest, over and over, as she stared across the room. Olivia said nothing before pulling a square piece of paper from the leather portfolio she'd brought. Then she folded one corner to the other side as she began creating an origami crane. It's what her therapist had taught her during the eighteen-month investigation and trial of her cousin Emily's murderer.

After Olivia had folded a crane, she set it on the bedside table and began folding another. And another. Eventually, Anja's gaze shifted to her hands.

"What are you making?" she asked.

"Cranes. Would you like to learn how?"

"Yes."

For the next ten minutes, Olivia patiently taught Anja the complex, multi-step process to fold a paper crane. It was a bit lumpy and misshapen, but she'd gotten all of the steps down.

"I saw him before," said Anja afterwards without looking at Olivia. She swallowed hard. "The man who called me whore and urged the others to rape me."

"He spoke to you in German?" asked Olivia.

Anja nodded. "At Tajine Barakah. It's a Moroccan takeout place in my neighborhood."

Olivia's nerves buzzed. Alami had called Tajine Barakah numerous times during their surveillance. "Blessed Stew" had seemed a flippant—and non-zealous—allusion to the Muslim equivalent of the Holy Spirit. They'd vetted the staff and the regular customers. None had any links with extremists.

It appeared they'd missed something.

Olivia spent another few minutes with Anja, promising to check on her when she had time. Then she left the hospital and headed toward Tajine Barakah, calling Thomas on the way.

But when he picked up, he delivered news before she could speak.

"Raif says he sent money to a broker in Brussels on behalf of a friend of Alami's."

"Anja recognized one of the men from her neighborhood Moroccan takeout place."

"Who?"

"The rape victim," said Olivia, letting exasperation tinge her voice. "It was Tajine Barakah. That's one of the places Alami ordered food from every few weeks. The last time was after his visit to Belgium."

"You were right. There's a connection between the rapes and the bombing on the Christmas market."

"You don't have to sound so reluctant to admit it."

Thomas sighed. Olivia imagined him running his fingers through his hair. "That's fair. Look, I'm sorry, Olivia. I'm just a little stressed. I should've seen the signs."

"You *did* see the signs, Thomas," said Olivia, parking on a street two blocks from Tajine Barakah. "That's why you ordered the team to follow him. But you're not Nostradamus. You can't predict the actual target and time without enough evidence."

"Speaking of evidence, Monica has correlated Alami's Belgium trip to one of the last sightings of him. And Bryce has identified the backpack bomber as Sadik Bennani, a Belgian citizen. We leave in an hour for Brussels."

"Copy that," said Olivia, jogging toward the Moroccan restaurant.

She had a few minutes to query the restaurant's staff about the German-speaking instigator who'd managed to avoid the CCTV cameras on the plaza. Something told Olivia that she'd learn more than whether he preferred lamb or chicken in his tajine.

Two-and-a-half hours later, the team landed at a private airstrip outside Brussels where they were met by Belgian foreign intelligence and a local CIA field officer, Trent Jones. It was mid-afternoon, nearly twenty-four hours after the bomb had exploded. Olivia should have been tired, but she was still wired from the assault inside the Kaiser Wilhem Memorial Church. It was the first time that she'd killed anyone since the Ibiza terrorist attack almost four years before, when she'd still been an innocent pre-med student fighting for her life. Having been stabbed in the process, she'd had little time to relive the moment until weeks later, safe at home in her bed for the nightmares. The fact that she'd taken human lives less than a day ago bubbled underneath the anxiety about a new attack and her determination to stop it.

Trent's voice focused her attention on the matter at hand.

"We've set up a tac center northeast of the city center," he said as they jogged to the waiting transport. "Marco's team has analyzed the target's previous visit to Brussels and Bennani's last-known address. We've narrowed down a five-kilometer area that covers all of Schaerbeek and some of the surrounding municipalities where we think Alami and Bennani are most likely hiding."

Thomas nodded. He turned towards the team intending to speak when Trent continued. "And we're starting to get some local chatter from our informants that something big has been planned to make up for the miss in Berlin."

Olivia's nerves, already on edge, tightened. Flashes of the Ibiza beach as the terrorists walked through the crowd of tourists, gunning them down, played before her mind's eye in kaleidoscopic frenzy. The vivid image of a stony-faced man knifing a nearby young couple, who'd just gotten engaged in a dramatic scene fifteen minutes before, sent terror washing through her.

Thomas, who knew her back story, glanced at her as the group halted next to two black BMW SUVs. "You okay, Markham?"

Mutely, Olivia nodded, fingering the St. Michael medal on her chest. *Sensei* Mark's voice, reminding her to breathe through the pain, evaporated the terror. Wellbeing and calm clarified her thoughts.

"Well, then," said Thomas, looking off into the distance toward the lights of Brussels, twinkling now as evening encroached. Above them, the pale sky faded into watery orange.

Just an ordinary evening in late November where people commuted home to their families and shopped for Christmas gifts. If they did their jobs, no one in the European capital would ever know that mortal danger had faced them.

Thomas brought his penetrating gaze back to the team. "No more fuckups. Or this time innocent civilians will die."

Olivia knew that at least part of that command had been directed at her.

THREE

The initial push to track and capture Alami and Bennani before they detonated another bomb waned as the team's search dragged over the next week. Everyone's nerves sharpened to a razor's edge as the local chatter about an imminent threat intensified without any new leads. No one on the team or their Belgian counterparts joked. Non-essential conversations and activities were kept to a minimum, and the only time someone left the TOC or the field was to use the toilet, shower, or sleep for a few short hours. Meals consisted of cold foods eaten in front of a screen or in the front seat of a vehicle.

What had started out as a sprint had morphed into a longer run. No one expected a marathon, however. So, they ate and slept when they could. Thomas had a punching bag and a pullup bar installed in an unused corner and issued sleep masks and earplugs.

Strangely, Olivia's anxiety diminished along with the strain. Her mind filled with crystal calm. She needed less sleep. Her normal, healthy appetite disappeared, and she often forgot to eat. Given the surly responses from the others, she suspected that they'd noticed and resented her unflagging spirit and consistent energy. She tried to stay out of their field of vision as much as possible as a result.

She'd had an idea blossom when Thomas allowed Bryce to order the team takeout, their first hot meal in a week. She'd just moved to the relevant physical files when Thomas let out a harsh breath as a prelude to speaking.

"When are these fuckers going to show their faces?" he said. His own face looked haggard and rough with enough stubble to predict the shape of his beard. Apparently, shaving took too much time.

Bryce, noise-cancelling headphones slung around his neck, looked at their team leader. "Boss, there's some interesting news going around Marco's office. Seems a local police inspector had a walk-in two days ago with a very interesting tale."

"Tell me." Thomas, his gaze sharpening, moved to stand next to Bryce. He crossed his arms.

Monica swiveled in her chair. She was one of those people who had to exercise to maintain an even keel. She hadn't been able to run in the mornings, and it showed in her scowl and puffy features.

Olivia set the pen in her hand on top of her notes, focusing on Bryce's news.

"Get this. A Belgian citizen of Moroccan descent, a woman named Anika Radi, said that she's seen Alami and Bennani among the homeless in Etterbeek."

The municipality of Etterbeek, where many European institutions had offices and half the population came from other countries, bordered Schaerbeek. It was expensive, densely populated, and moderately afflicted with crime.

"Right under everyone's noses, in the heart of the EU's governing city," said Monica. "That checks out."

Thomas ignored her sarcastic remark, instead directing a question to Bryce. "What makes you think her information is authentic as opposed to all of the other false tips we've received after Bennani's name and picture made it into the media?"

Bryce, the least cranky of Olivia's teammates, lifted a nonchalant shoulder. When he spoke, his heightened Texas twang hinted at hidden stress, however.

"She's been letting Bennani's cousin stay with her for the past couple of months. *That* checks out." He shot a glance at Monica that undercut his apparent easygoing attitude.

"Why did it take so long for Marco to learn about Radi?" asked Olivia as she opened the drawer where she kept a leather ammo belt and spare clips for her Sig Sauer 9mm.

Meaning *why did it take so long for the Belgians to get this bit of intel?*

She checked the clip in her weapon and then slipped an extra clip into her back pocket. It wasn't likely they'd be going into an ambush, but it paid to be prepared.

Bryce shifted in his seat, his lanky form transforming from relaxed to alert in seconds. "Partly because the local police have a beef with Belgian intelligence," he said, "partly because Radi, an immigrant, had reticence about going to the police. She waited to speak to a female officer, who unfortunately didn't find her story credible."

"No shit," said Monica.

Bryce glared at her but continued his account. "The police translator also mistranslated Radi's description of where Alami and Bennani pitched their tent. There was nothing there."

"Let me guess," said Olivia, looking up. "The police translator speaks MSA, not Darija."

MSA, or Modern Standard Arabic, was the *lingua franca* of the Muslim world, useful for Arabic speakers from all over, but very different from Maghrebi, which many other dialect speakers found almost unintelligible. Even Maghrebi had regional variants that could confuse a Belgian translator.

Thomas, watching Olivia as she got ready to go into the field, asked, "You learn something to back up Radi's story?"

Olivia stood upright, ready to go. "The takeout place, Tajine Barakah?"

He nodded, impatience flitting across his face.

"I took a look at the transcripts from all the phone orders Alami made, especially the last one before he took his trip to Belgium. He sent it to a nonexistent Berlin address. So I analyzed all of the food orders and Alami's movements. That's when I realized he'd been getting coded messages this whole time." She glanced at Monica. "Right under *our* noses."

Thomas anticipated where Olivia was going with this. "The nonexistent Berlin address matches the location that Radi saw Alami and Bennani here in Brussels."

Olivia nodded. "There's more. As best I can determine, Alami and Bennani have been ordered to observe Ashura by emulating Husayn ibn Ali."

Husayn ibn Ali, the Prophet Muhammed's grandson, had been martyred. Ashura, the tenth day of the first Islamic month of Muharram, commemorated his beheading.

This year the holy day fell on December 4th—two days away.

Bryce stood. "Liv and I can interview Radi. Marco's team hasn't yet realized the tip's got legs. We can get there before they do."

Thomas, his lips compressed in a hard line, dipped his chin in approval.

They all knew that the Belgian police had likely missed some salient details.

"I take it you got the correct description of Alami and Bennani's camp site?" he asked Olivia, who nodded. "Give us the details. Monica and I will scout the neighborhood around the homeless encampment and meet you back here in two hours. We'll go over logistics then."

Bryce said nothing as he and Olivia tugged on their winter jackets to head towards Schaerbeek where Radi lived in a furnished one-bedroom apartment on the eleventh floor of a monolithic apartment building. Bennani's cousin must sleep on the sofa. They'd have to be careful approaching Radi, but the police file said the cousin worked nights cleaning office buildings.

However, after they got into the car, Bryce said, "You took a look at the transcripts because your rape victim mentioned Tajine Barakah, didn't she?"

Olivia, who drove, didn't look at him. "Yes" was all she allowed herself to say.

"Don't get me wrong, Sweetheart," said Bryce, the endearment natural and not condescending. Olivia rather liked it when he used it. She hadn't been called *sweetheart* since she'd lived at home. "I'm on your side. But I've worked with Thomas for a while now. He's not a bad guy, he's just laser focused on the job. I know you didn't mention the connection you found for a reason. I want to confirm that your instinct was right."

Now Olivia shot Bryce a quick glance. Bryce's serious face showed no threat.

"Is my instinct to trust you right then?" she asked.

"Absolutely. I would never disrupt the smooth functioning of this team by telling the boss that his girlfriend has gone behind his back and pursued her own agenda."

Olivia's heart lurched at that. She and Thomas had been so careful. Too careful, she saw now. Their public interactions must have an unnatural quality, an awkwardness that a sensitive person would pick up on.

Or any trained operative—especially one who depended on his teammates to stay focused.

They didn't speak again before arriving at the apartment. By tacit agreement, Bryce remained outside on watch while Olivia, a less threatening persona, approached the informant's apartment.

After Olivia's quick knock, Anika Radi, wearing a wary expression, opened her door a hands' width. In her twenties now, she'd moved to Belgium with her family more than a decade before. After university, she'd taken an office job with Atrium, the regional trade agency that helped entrepreneurs and small businesses in Brussels, where her French fluency and connections in the Moroccan community helped make her an attractive employee.

Smiling warmly, Olivia introduced herself in French as a member of the Belgian federal police, brandishing an authentic-looking ID. Radi's closed expression opened to show relief, though not trust. Marco's group had yet to interview her, and she clearly needed someone in law enforcement to take her seriously.

Anika invited Olivia into her neat home, which was furnished with a fusion of Belgian and Moroccan styles. She prepared Maghrebi mint tea in the traditional manner using fresh mint and high-quality gunpowder-tea pellets. Olivia waited until they'd consumed the customary three cups of tea before querying about Alami and Bennani.

It seemed appropriate. A Maghrebi proverb said that the third cup was as bitter as death.

"Please tell me everything that you told my colleagues in the police department as if it is the first time you tell this story," said Olivia, leaning a little toward the other woman. "Because, between you and me, they aren't so competent. That's why it took so long for us to follow up with you."

Anika nodded. She rotated her glass cup between her palms as she repeated her story. Olivia transcribed her account, though the local police had taken meticulous notes. It was important for Anika to see that Olivia took her story seriously. And Olivia had learned long ago to do her own legwork.

"Can you please describe Hafid and Sadik when you saw them? What were they wearing?"

Anika shrugged. "Nothing in particular. Dark-gray hoodies under black, puffy jackets, jeans, and sneakers, you know the kind that Americans wear, the ones with the big check mark."

"You mean this brand?" asked Olivia, showing Anika an image on her cellphone.

Anika nodded again. "Yes, only not black. These were bright red. I heard him tell Zahra that they are called 'Reign of Blood' like their mission among the *kafir*. He laughed about it." She shuddered and sipped the last of her tea.

The back of Olivia's neck tingled. This was the missing detail that the Belgians hadn't gotten. It would make identifying the *jihadis* on the street faster despite their clever hiding plan. Alami's arrogant vanity would cost him.

After another twenty minutes clarifying details and asking more about Zahra, Bennani's cousin, she thanked Anika for her time and the tea.

As she rose to go, Anika surprised her by asking, "How can a beautiful young woman like you be a federal agent and chase after men who want to see the world burn? Aren't you afraid of them?"

Olivia paused as she tucked her notebook into her jacket pocket.

"Yes," she said. "But, like you"—here she nodded at Anika—"I can't wait in the shadows for men to make the world safer for women and children. I must use the talents and gifts I've been given or I can't live with myself."

As Olivia said this, her St. Michael medal heated. She touched it with a fingertip as a premonition washed through her.

When Bryce and Olivia returned to the TOC, Thomas waited for them with news and photos. He'd left Monica to surveil the group of homeless people lying under the overhang of a commercial building in the heart of Etterbeek where Anika had visited Alami with Zahra. Most of them appeared to be Eastern European, possibly Polish, but there were smaller clusters of two or three individuals on the margins of the main group. These included pairs of men of indeterminate background. Unfortunately, the Belgian police had begun moving the homeless into shelters overnight as the temperatures plummeted, and it was only a matter of time before they got to this encampment, forcing the targets to scatter or go into hiding elsewhere.

Fortunately, Olivia had the identifying detail that would make their mission a bit easier.

She pointed to a photo on the side of the pile showing two huddled figures with faces hidden inside hoods. One of them wore a bright red pair of sneakers with the trademark swoosh of the popular American shoe brand.

"Those two men. That's our target. Alami's wearing the red sneakers."

Thomas, who leaned over the table next to her, glanced at her. "Good work, Markham. Those jackets also look unnaturally bulky for their frames. We have to assume that they're wearing their bomb vests night and day until Ashura." He updated Monica, who would now find and watch the two *jihadis*.

Trent arrived as they readied for the field. For this operation, he would act as their handler, coordinating with Marco's team and getting regular status updates from his police contact. Prior to their update, the Belgian intelligence officer had opted to follow Bennani's cousin in hopes of her leading his team back to the two *jihadis*. Once Thomas notified him of their findings, Marco left a tail on the cousin and a tap on her cellphone.

Monica called Olivia as Thomas reviewed logistics with the assembled joint team.

"We've got a problem," she said.

Olivia caught Thomas's glance and gave a sharp nod at his questioning expression as she said, "Tell me."

"The leader of the Polish faction and Alami are about to go kinetic. One of the Polish women got too close to the targets. Now Alami and the alpha male of the Poles are doing a dominance dance. It's only a matter of time before it escalates from words to weapons."

"Copy that." Olivia ended the call. Thomas had stopped the briefing and waited for her pronouncement. "Jade Doll says it's time to gear up and ride. Alami and Bennani have lost cover among the homeless."

"The Belgian police have been notified," said Trent from the doorway. "They're sending a couple of units."

Better and better. If the police got there before they did, the likelihood that Alami and Bennani detonated their vests went from highly likely to a hundred percent.

The two teams sprinted to their vehicles, armored BMW SUVs that could withstand machine-gun fire but not explosives. Given the locale, they were a common sight.

The homeless encampment was on the southeast side of the Parc du Cinquantenaire, a little more than three kilometers from the TOC in the center of Schaerbeek. At this time of the day, late evening, the drive would take fifteen minutes for the average driver.

They managed it in nine.

Even so, the Belgian police arrived before they did.

As the operatives ran toward the scene, taking cover behind parked cars on either end of the street, the grim tableau before them told a shocking story.

The Polish leader who'd engaged in a shoving match with Alami lay sprawled on the sidewalk under the overhang, bleeding out in the crisp December air from a stab wound. A woman wearing stained and worn winter clothing knelt at his side, sobbing.

Two pairs of police officers encircled Alami and Bennani at a distance of twenty meters, weapons in their hands, their gazes locked on the two men and yelling conflicting commands to drop the knife or kneel.

Alami and Bennani stood shoulder-to-shoulder in the street in front of the camp, the personal belongings of some two-dozen homeless individuals scattered like detritus around them. Neither man showed any fear or uncertainty but watched the police officers with the stillness of those who waited for the signal to act.

The remaining homeless people watched, the flat resignation on their faces its own kind of horror.

Olivia glimpsed Monica easing between parked cars, her weapon raised in a two-handed grip as she sought an opening to take out the would-be bombers.

"I've got the shot on Alami," she said through comms.

Warning shrieked through Olivia.

And then Alami and Bennani detonated their vests.

Olivia, beside a heavy Mercedes sedan that rocked with the force of the blast, stumbled and fell against the car's hood before landing on a knee, hard. Glass shattered all around her, cascading to the pavement in a deadly rain. All other sounds disappeared in a white vacuum, even the low-level hum that seemed to link Olivia's every breath. Streetlights winked out.

Harsh, chaotic sound returned in a cold rush: car alarms blaring, sobbing and moaning, incoherent babble.

Olivia pushed to her feet, and, propping her hands on the Mercedes, looked into the street where the drama had played out.

An almost-indescribable atrocity met her gaze.

None of the people—including Monica—who'd been there moments before existed anymore.

Instead, debris had blown across the pavement like confetti from a giant's celebration. The lower stories of the commercial building had disintegrated along their outside walls, sliding into messy piles on the ground below. Here and there, Olivia saw body parts, including Bennani's head, which had been popped from his body and thrown thirty meters. All of the closest streetlights had been destroyed, and only indirect light from either side of the street lit the macabre scene.

Shoving away from the Mercedes, Olivia stumbled toward the last place she'd seen Monica. Her injured right knee buckled, and she almost fell but managed to catch herself.

That's when her gaze snagged on what was left of Monica, who'd been thrown against a parked Audi. Her friend, the one who'd had Olivia's back since their first mission together in D.C., lay at an awkward angle against the car's front tire, one arm and most of both legs missing. Her head rested on her shoulder, the long brown hair silky against her cheeks and her eyes closed as if she only napped.

Olivia's brilliant lead hadn't saved her friend or prevented tragedy.

When Thomas came beside her and took her hand, Olivia looked at him through blurry eyes. He reached out with his free hand and gently wiped her cheeks with his thumb.

At that moment, Olivia realized that she was crying.

FOUR

The three men, all refugees from the civil war in Syria, wandered along the Sonnenallee, or Sun Alley, in southeast Berlin. The four-lane boulevard had come to be known as 'Arab Street' for its influx of immigrants, though this was something of a misnomer because Turks made up the largest percentage of non-European inhabitants. They'd only been in Germany for a few months, but none of the men liked the climate in this northern country so unlike their own. At least they had the familiar food shops and customs of their homeland in this neighborhood, thankfully nearly free of Christmas decorations.

Akram, an anxious man whose hands flitted around his face whenever he spoke, said, "Have you heard what happened to our Moroccan brethren, the ones with us at the *kafir* market?"

Fadhi shook his head. Onsi, who'd glanced aside at some German women walking in the opposite direction, looked back at the other two.

"Those fools? I hope they blow themselves up. I would rather live among the unbelievers than sacrifice myself to leave only a puddle on the pavement. If I'd wanted to die, I would have let Assad gas me."

As he spoke, they walked past a *shisha* shop where men sucked on water pipes, and fragrant smoke flavored with vanilla, honey, figs, and mint wafted on the chill late-December evening. Up ahead, a stretch of empty storefronts loomed. Although more of their Syrian compatriots arrived every day, adding life to the Sonnenallee, it was as yet filled with vast opportunity for the thousands of Syrian refugees streaming into Europe through Turkey.

Akram flinched at Onsi's comment and looked around, as if he feared Assad's agents had followed them to Berlin.

When he brought his gaze back to his friends, former shopkeepers in Damascus who'd escaped with little more than the clothes on their backs, the whites of his eyes shone in the streetlight.

"You may not get a choice," said Akram. "Those 'fools' as you call them were found this morning by the *polizei*, beaten and tied to a bench. Worse, some whisper that they had their mouths swabbed for their DNA."

Onsi halted. Fadhi, the least talkative stopped with him. Akram walked several more meters before looking over his shoulder at his friends. He stopped, too.

"Why would an attacker swab them for their DNA?" Onsi said, scoffing. "You've been watching too many Western TV shows. It's turning your brain into *mamounieh*."

Fadhi snickered. The porridge had been a staple among the refugees as they traveled through Syria. Most avoided it now from the memories it evoked.

"Because she wanted to link the Maghrebi 'fools' to the attack on the German woman at the Christmas market," said a voice in Levantine Arabic behind them. "And now she's going to do the same to you."

Onsi, Fadhi, and Akram swiveled to look at the beautiful blonde behind them. Her haunting blue-gray eyes promised pain. The gun in her hands assured that she would deliver it.

Onsi laughed again. And then he rushed her. He was like that, impulsive.

The blonde didn't waver or recoil. Instead, she stepped forward and slid sideways as Onsi reached her, her nearest elbow whipping into his head. As Onsi lurched, his arms flapping as he tried to regain his balance, she stomped the back of his nearest knee. He crumpled.

But Fadhi didn't wait for his childhood friend to go down. He launched himself at the woman as soon as her elbow struck Onsi, knocking the gun from her hand as she kicked. It landed at Akram's feet.

He scooped it up, frantically trying to get his finger inside the trigger and palm on the grip.

Meanwhile, the agile woman ducked under Fadhi's arm, which she grabbed with her hands, now empty, and wrenched up his back.

Fadhi screamed but continued to struggle. The woman's knee buckled unexpectedly, and the elbow of Fadhi's free arm caught her on the cheekbone. Her head snapped back, but she retained hold of his arm. Stepping toward Fadhi, she pivoted him to face Akram, whose hand shook violently as he pointed the gun's muzzle at them.

"I wouldn't pull the trigger if I were you," she said. "You'll either shoot your friend or the recoil will throw your aim. Either way, then you'll have to deal with me, and I won't be so kind to someone who tried to shoot me."

Akram heard the truth in her voice. A bead of sweat slid down his temple despite the cold air. He swallowed, hard. His hand shook harder.

Onsi made up Akram's mind for him by lurching to his feet.

The blonde shoved Fadhi at Onsi, who fell under the sudden weight. Akram's finger pulled the trigger before he could reconsider. The gun bucked, sending the bullet into the window of the dark storefront beside them. And then she tackled him, bringing him down to the pavement, rolling under him with her legs around his mid-section and an arm choking his throat.

As blackness dissolved Akram's sight, the she-demon whispered into his ear. "Hope you like prison, you cowardly piece of shit."

Olivia looked in the mirror at the darkening bruise on her cheekbone. She healed insanely fast, but it would still be visible when she met Thomas later for dinner. He was already suspicious of the time she'd requested off after the post-mortem of the Belgian operation, though no one questioned her desire to escort Monica's remains back to the U.S. What would he think when he saw the bruises and scrapes on her from taking Anja's Syrian attackers down? Perhaps she could convince him that her wonky knee had handicapped her during sparring. It was close enough to the truth, something the CIA had taught her worked when sold with confidence.

Today had been the first time that she'd been in the Berlin station since Brussels, in fact. The team had met with one of the Company's target-recovery experts, a man named Miles Baxter. Baxter had a reputation for suffering no fools and anticipating exactly where and how individuals escaped. Thomas not only respected him, he envied Baxter. And now he resented the necessity of bringing the snatch-and-grab professional onboard his mission.

That's because it had turned out that Raif Al Numan, his *hawaladar* asset, had been playing both sides. The canny Syrian money broker had been in the wind ever since Brussels, long before Homeland Security picked up his parents in the U.S. Unfortunately for Raif, he'd been skimming money and sending it to those parents, who'd not been as careful with it as he'd likely warned them, attracting attention from both the U.S. intelligence services and the terrorists for whom he'd been funneling money.

Sighing, Olivia brushed her hair back into a ponytail. As she did, the overhead light glinted off the engagement ring that she still wore. She wondered when they'd give up the charade. Clearly not for a while given that Thomas's request to go after Raif had been denied. Instead, the station chief wanted Thomas's team to work German connections regarding a rumored arms shipment destined for another terrorist cell in France. They got the mission brief today after handing Raif's capture off to Baxter, along with a new teammate named Hanna. Taking into account the urgency and intercontinental nature of the new mission, Olivia suspected that they'd be on the move from Berlin in the next few days, their married cover intact.

The clock was ticking on her unsanctioned investigation into Mr. X's identity and her roundup of Anja's rapists.

Olivia pulled on a demure pair of black slacks and an off-white cashmere sweater, her attire as the wealthy young wife of an American import-export entrepreneur—the ideal business cover for operatives who traveled. She twisted the ponytail into an expert French chignon, deftly tucking the ends under with hairpins before checking her efforts in the mirrors around her. A pair of diamond-drop earrings, tasteful makeup, and designer riding boots added to the elegant image and aged her a few years.

She frowned at that thought.

She'd always been studious and serious and taken seriously by those who knew her, despite her youth and beauty. She hadn't learned to despise either until she'd started working cover identities that didn't rely on being a student. And then she found that others often didn't treat her respectfully or thoughtfully.

It wasn't her teammates, who knew her, or even most of the people with whom she came into contact in the CIA field offices. Those people respected skill, judgment, and experience. She'd shown to have all of those.

No, it was usually the average people that she met, the ones who didn't accept her cover so readily and treated her almost as invisible. That was a fine result at times, letting her leverage their underestimation. But more often than not, it hampered her work.

The new woman, Hanna, had been at the Agency longer and had a decade of field experience. With her shoulder-length dark hair and hard gray eyes that saw everything, Olivia imagined that she didn't need little tricks of makeup and clothes to add mystique and glamour to her cover roles. No one would dare ignore or underestimate Hanna, least of all Olivia.

Hanna had jumped right into the mission briefing as if she'd been on the team all along. She hadn't been afraid to critique Thomas or assert that her contact at a Berlin-based Russian organized-crime gang knew or could find out about all the illegal arms that came into or left the city. Thomas, who didn't speak Russian, had given Hanna leeway to work the contact before they committed to any other plans.

Olivia had watched the interaction, stunned at Thomas's deferral to the newcomer. He usually asserted operational dominance whenever working with someone new, regardless of their background or role.

Now the memory of the glittering appreciation in his eyes and Hanna's cool disregard sent a thrum of worry through Olivia.

Olivia shrugged on her cover's fine wool jacket and grabbed the keys to the Audi sedan assigned to her before looking around the luxury flat that she and Thomas shared. She'd left no evidence of her vigilante activities, including the weapon that Bryce had sourced for her from a former Army buddy. The clothes had gone into a dumpster, and the zip ties and thumb drive with the police files and her notes into a rented locker at the central bus station.

Glancing at her watch, she saw that she had time to check on her guest.

She dialed Tajine Barakah as she locked the flat's door, ordering Alami's favorite dish to be delivered to an empty store on the Sonnenallee where she'd stored the bound Akram. Onsi and Fadhi had, unfortunately for them, been picked up by local law enforcement along with enough details to connect them to Anja's rape. Just to make sure that Mr. X understood that he'd been implicated along with them, she'd left his mobile phone number for the police.

After Olivia arrived on 'Arab Street,' she parked a block down where she could watch the front of the store. She'd prepped the space by installing IP security cameras with motion sensors inside and over the back door, in case Mr. X chose not to enter by the front. Then she'd left a mobile hotspot plugged into an outlet in a nearby café to stream video.

The sun had set while she drove. By now, darkness and the bright lights from the surrounding businesses gave her cover to watch unseen by any cursory observation. Unless Mr. X had someone on the Berlin police force or connected the delivery order with her visit to Tajine Barakah weeks ago, which Olivia highly doubted, he wouldn't have a description of her to look for anyway. It was the best she could do solo.

Olivia looked down where the weapon Bryce had gotten her lay on the passenger seat. The provenance of the German-made Walther P99 9mm handgun couldn't be traced, yet numerous German police departments and the Finnish special forces and miliary police carried the same gun. Its use suggested someone other than an American intelligence operative.

Bryce hadn't asked any questions, but Olivia knew that simply asking for an untraceable weapon told him all he needed to know.

She looked back out the windshield, her fingers tapping on the steering wheel.

It wouldn't do to rely on Bryce or anyone in the field office for support or resources when she colored outside the lines. She needed to start building her own resources. Every good field officer had them for those times when the CIA either didn't or couldn't help.

Olivia checked her watch.

Something was wrong. More than thirty minutes had passed since she phoned in the order to Tajine Barakah. Had she been wrong about

Mr. X being the substitute delivery driver the restaurant owner had identified on her previous trip? What if he no longer listened for the code now that Alami and Bennani were dead?

She shook her head. No, that man was controlling and micro-managing, she was sure of it. He also had multiple other assets he was grooming from the shadows for other attacks. *That* she'd bet her last dollar on. He might have switched codewords and restaurants, but he would keep track of previous communication channels—especially after she tweaked his nose via the police this morning.

Olivia tapped the security-cam app on her smartphone.

That was odd. The personal WiFi brick tethered to her phone that relayed video from the cameras had gone inactive. Someone had found and unplugged it.

She sighed.

It had been a risk, but she'd scouted the location days ago and gained access to a storage space where she could hide the device plugged into an unused and blocked outlet. An employee must have found it since she last checked on Akram.

Stuffing the Walther into her coat pocket, Olivia got out of the sedan, checking the surrounding blocks for any sign that she had a tail or that a lookout had been posted. She saw nothing unusual, but the medal on her chest heated. The hairs on the back of her neck shivered.

She touched the medal before sliding her hand into her pocket and gripping the gun. As she walked toward the empty store, the crawling sensation increased. Someone was watching her. She was sure of it.

Instead of approaching the door, she walked past without a glance and farther down the block to a bustling *shawarma* takeout restaurant. She'd created a chokepoint that would keep anyone tailing her outside. That was all well and good, but it meant she had to come up with a new plan.

Somehow Mr. X had arrived before her and found a vantage point from which to watch the empty store.

Olivia was debating what to do when a voice behind her said in German, "You don't look particularly threatening." Then the voice switched to the flavor of Maghrebi Arabic she'd heard weeks ago at the Christmas market. "Perhaps you are a demon who compelled Onsi, Fadhi, and Akram to tie themselves up."

Olivia's heart squeezed in her chest as if a giant wrung out a dishrag. She'd never expected Mr. X to be *in* the *shawarma* restaurant waiting for her.

She should have anticipated that he'd have a team. The skilled deployment of assets on Breitscheidplatz had shown that the terrorist handler employed sophisticated tactics.

She touched her medal, and, forcing her breathing to remain steady, turned to face her antagonist.

The middle-aged man before her had a familiar seamed face that projected sorrow at odds with the malicious gleam in his medium-brown eyes. Although his white hair and beard suggested age, his wiry form and muscled forearms conveyed an impression of strength and vitality. He wore a heavy wool *djellaba*, the traditional Moroccan outer hooded robe, baggy *qandrissi* pants, and a white *taqiyah* skullcap. He looked like he'd be at home in the Sahara, not wintry Berlin.

Olivia, pulling her shoulders back and lifting her chin, addressed his mockery of her and his minions. "*You* don't look particularly threatening, and yet you are," she said in Maghrebi Arabic. "You're definitely a *shaitan* who whispers evil to the believers, inciting them to sin through rape and massacre. Would you like to see how I 'compelled' your minions into police custody? I can do the same for you."

Clenching his jaw, her opponent narrowed his eyes and hissed at her description. "How dare you speak those words to me, you blasphemous ape?"

Olivia's anger flared at his sneering contempt and the nasty characterization. Stepping into his personal space, she leaned closer to his face, forcing him to pull away.

"I dare."

"You won't find it so easy to overcome me, demon," he said.

That's when their surroundings penetrated Olivia's anger. Besides the *shawarma* restaurant's customers, which included a mother and her two young sons, three large men stood along the perimeter of the small dining space, their hands crossed and watching her and their master with hooded eyes.

She'd created a chokepoint, all right. For herself.

She was trapped.

And then Thomas entered the restaurant, smiling at Olivia. Bryce and Hanna came behind, holding hands but clearly with Thomas. The tension in the restaurant declined. A notch.

"Darling!" said Thomas in German as he reached Olivia, drawing her into his arms and blocking Mr. X's view of her. "I'm so sorry that we're late." He pulled her hand into his as he stepped back. "Did you order already? I hope not because I've changed my mind. I'd rather eat *schnitzel*."

Olivia, trained to pivot as fieldwork required, shook her head. "I was just discussing the menu with this man, but nothing that he suggests suits me. We can go elsewhere for dinner."

"Sounds good," said Thomas. He lifted his chin at Bryce and Hanna. "Let's go back to the city center. I know a good *schnitzel* place."

Murmuring acquiescence, Bryce and Hanna filed in behind them, guarding their back as they exited before the other couple peeled off to get into the 10-year-old Opel sedan the team had driven there.

Olivia's breathing eased a little as Thomas escorted her back to the Audi.

Only to catch in her chest again a minute later when Thomas, now behind the wheel, glared over at her. And then, shocking her, he reached out and touched her bruised cheek.

When he spoke, his rough voice conveyed strong emotion. "Why are you in this neighborhood about to get your ass kicked by some Moroccan goons?"

Olivia bristled, but she knew that Thomas had a right to be angry. "That was Alami's handler," she said, struggling to keep her voice even. "Tajine Barakah used him as a substitute delivery driver."

Thomas blinked at that before running a hand through his hair. He sighed and started the car. They drove in silence for several long moments before he said, "It doesn't matter, Liv. He's not our mission now." He glanced at her. "This isn't about intuition or interviewing witnesses this time, is it."

A statement, not a question.

"How much do you know?"

He had to know quite a bit to have brought the team to her rescue when he did.

"Enough. Enough to know that this can't go on. Liv, you have to focus on Company business, not this obsession with getting justice for a rape victim."

"What if they're the same? C'mon, Thomas, you know as well as I do that this guy isn't going to stop. He's prepping other disaffected Muslims *right now*."

"And you found him by beating the crap out of some of them. You're either going to get yourself seriously hurt or you're going to compromise your cover here. You should have brought what you had to me, your team leader, not gone after Alami's handler on your own."

"Just like you brought your request to go after Raif to Jordan?" Jordan was the Berlin station chief. "How'd that work out for you? Or how about Anika who was arrested by the Belgians for sheltering Zahra despite the fact that she did the right thing and went to the authorities with what she knew? How does that make sense?" Olivia put her hand on Thomas's arm. "What are we doing this for if it's not to make women like Anja and Anika safe?"

He looked over at her, his eyes narrowing. "This isn't useful to us, Liv. I can't and *won't* continue making sure you're safe while you go off the reservation. We need to gather actionable intel without compromising strategic objectives."

Olivia sat in silence as he drove. What was there to say? That, unlike him, she wasn't going to back down now?

Finally, Thomas said, "I've put in a request to transfer you to the Prague field station where the *jihadis*, whoever they are, won't recognize you, and you can refocus on the mission. And so can my team. You leave in three days."

Shock washed over Olivia at his unexpected words. "What about us?" she asked in a low voice.

"Us? There's no 'us,' Olivia. There's only the Agency and the War on Terror."

FIVE

Prague in March reminded Olivia of New England in March—well, the weather and landscape, anyway. Boston's colonial architecture, though historic for the U.S., paled in comparison to the dramatic architecture of Prague, whose red-roofed buildings had miraculously escaped bombing in World War Two. In fact, the Old Town had scarcely changed in hundreds of years, and examples from all the major architectural ages, from Romanesque to Rococo, often stood side-by-side in its iconic streets.

Olivia tried to enjoy the city around her, tugging the collar of her London Fog overcoat up and imagining that she walked its streets during the height of the Cold War, when being a field operative meant carrying briefcases with false bottoms and umbrellas with ricin-laced bullets in their modified handles. As a woman, her role in spying would depend on cat-and-mouse intrigue, smoky clubs, and mysterious strangers. A romantic and alluring dance along an assassin's razor's edge, not a gritty and violent chase of dead-eyed mass murderers.

It didn't help much.

Probably because there was no romance or real intrigue in her current mission, let alone any real danger.

When she'd landed in Prague, the local station chief had seemed both perplexed and annoyed at her sudden addition to his roster. He'd sent Olivia to the records room and told her to go through all of the graymail—that is, the unsolicited correspondence that the Prague station had received in the past two years that alluded to or in some cases mentioned outright Agency secrets in the region. Ever since the Mohamed Atta fiasco almost a decade before when Czech intelligence had mistaken a similarly named Pakistani for the 9-11 terrorist—which fed directly into the rationale for the U.S. going to war in Iraq—reams of letter writers had claimed (without merit as far as Olivia could tell) to have insider knowledge of other Agency missteps of similar magnitude. Though the likelihood that something legitimate would come into the field station via this avenue was miniscule, the letters couldn't be dismissed or ignored.

Reviewing them was the perfect make-work task for a young intelligence officer, foisted on a new handler, who needed a bit of comeuppance.

That's why Olivia found herself strolling through the Easter market in the Old Town Square, wrestling with vivid flashbacks of the earlier mission at the Berlin Christmas market and wondering how long she had to continue wasting time on almost-certainly useless work. She'd read a handwritten letter from a young Russian woman who worked at the Russian embassy, long known in Western intelligence as a significant outpost for Russian foreign intelligence, now known as the SVR. Marina Orlova had claimed to have invaluable information regarding an upcoming black-market arms sale, but as a recent hire in the lowest-level administrative class, her fabulous tale didn't inspire confidence. Nevertheless, Olivia had contacted her and begun the agonizing recruitment of a skittish foreign asset.

Today she waited for Marina near a wooden shed selling *pomlázka* made of willow rods in a variety of lengths ranging from half a meter to two meters and decorated with colored ribbons at the end. The enterprising stall owner also sold spray bottles of perfume as a more genteel replacement for the bucket of cold water used in the traditional Easter Monday game. Rattles and painted eggs rounded out the offerings geared at tourists. Czechs themselves weren't particularly observant of the holiday.

"'Rejuvenator'?" asked Marina, translating the Czech word for the whips as she came to stand next to Olivia, who stood with her hands in her pockets. Marina pulled a package of cigarettes from her purse and, slipping one between her lips, lit it. "Being chased by vile little boys and spanked would hardly increase my fertility or desire to test it."

Olivia shrugged. She'd still not grown comfortable with the smoking she encountered in the Czech Republic, where a third of the population above the age of fifteen did it. A lot. Russia, Marina's native country, consumed nearly the same number of cigarettes. It made Olivia's approach more challenging when she had to conceal her distaste for the habit, but she was here in Prague to grow as an intelligence operative.

"I'm not a fan of abuse, but from what I can tell, it's a game more than anything else." Olivia looked at the other woman. "Just like this is a game, only I can't decide whether it's worth playing any more or not."

Marina looked at Olivia from the side of her eye as she reached for a *pomlázka* and caressed its satin ribbons. "Something tells me that you are the one to wield the whip, eh?"

Olivia sighed harshly. "Something tells me that this is your first job after university, isn't it, Marina? Trying to create a little excitement by pretending you know something you don't?"

Marina huffed and dropped the Czech souvenir. "You are one to talk. You cannot be much older than I am, and yet you treat me the same way they do. As if I have *borscht* between my ears."

Olivia regretted her intemperate words. Still, it was time to find out if this young Russian woman had actionable intelligence or not. Whether Marina would turn out to be worth cultivating long term hinged on the answer to that question. She turned to the other woman, slipping her arm through Marina's and guiding her away from the souvenir stall where their conversation wouldn't be overheard.

"Time to cut to the chase as we say in the U.S. Here's your final chance to convince me that you have anything of value to justify continuing our relationship. Unlike you, I have better things to do."

Marina stopped short before dropping her half-smoked cigarette to the pavement. She stamped and twisted her toe on it.

"Let me take a picture of us," she said, pulling her phone from her purse.

Olivia started to object; it wasn't a good idea for her to have photos with Russian embassy workers. However, before she could say anything, Marina lifted the phone. Instead of the phone's camera, an image from its gallery filled the screen. Olivia's protest died as she realized that Marina had taken a picture of herself with two older men, one of whom Olivia recognized from the Company's background files on the Russian embassy and recent visitors from the Motherland.

General Ilya Popov. And Marina had likely maneuvered him as she'd maneuvered Olivia.

"Nicely done," said Olivia. "Who is that with General Popov? And is that Bar Cohiba Atmosphere?" The private Cuban club known for its selection of imported cigars and high-end liquor appealed to a certain clientele.

Marina's sly grin as she slipped the phone into her purse told Olivia that she'd also been checking Olivia's *bona fides* with the image. If Olivia wasn't just a junior analyst who vetted the CIA mail, she'd know the value of Marina's access.

They continued walking toward Wenceslas Square where the noise from traffic and pedestrians guaranteed that their conversation would be essentially private.

Marina answered Olivia's question. "Indeed. General Popov has a terrible addiction to Cohiba Robusto cigars after he spent so many years in Cuba. And his friend Bogdi enjoys cognac and cocktails. Among other things."

Her innuendo along with the setting told Olivia all she needed to know.

"And you were there why?"

"Ah. I was, how shall I describe it? Like the concierge. I arranged payment for the cigars, cocktails, and ... entertainment."

"After a few drinks, you overheard something? Please tell me these men aren't that stupid," said Olivia. What she meant was *these men aren't that stupid, and neither am I.*

Marina shook her head, serious now. "No. They spoke in Polish. They didn't know that my grandmother is Polish."

Ah. That made sense. Russians with Polish ancestors liked to keep that connection quiet.

Olivia stopped in front of a store window, catching Marina's gaze in the reflection. "Go on."

"I overheard them discussing selling something to the highest bidder, whom Bogdi assured General Popov that he could supply. I thought nothing of it. Someone is always selling something on the black market, though usually it is we Russians who buy from others. But then I walked in on them when they clearly did not expect me. May I smoke?" she asked suddenly.

Olivia narrowed her eyes. She'd seen Marina's nervous glance over her shoulder and the way her fingers shook as she pulled the cigarette pack from her purse.

Swallowing her irritation, Olivia nodded. "Of course. Let's continue walking then."

As they began moving, Marina plucked a cigarette from the pack, set it between her lips, and lit it. Olivia exhaled, touching her St. Michael medal as her *sensei*'s voice whispered in her thoughts that not all tactics benefited from aggressive forward action.

"I heard the phrases 'the detonator' and 'the Syrian' and then Bogdi assured General Popov that nothing would be traced to him should it be used in Syria instead of Europe. If you ask me, it sounded like a desperate seduction, the way Bogdi wheedled and urged General Popov. Even though they were both quite drunk, they switched to Russian as soon as they realized I'd returned."

"But, of course, even if you didn't speak Polish, you would have understood 'detonator' as it's the same word in English," said Olivia, slowing.

"And Russian," added Marina. "But we pronounce it differently."

Olivia held Marina's gaze. "Are you sure they don't know that you overheard them? Because if they suspect you...." She let her words trail off as she glanced around, her senses on high alert.

Marina shook her head. When she spoke, she sounded bitter. "They suspect nothing. I have *borscht* for brains, remember? I had the hostess and the evening's 'entertainment' with me, and I made sure to seem anxious about whether General Popov would like his selection."

"Nevertheless, we need to be careful," said Olivia, picking up her pace, "especially as now you will need to find out more about this black-market deal."

For the next few weeks, Olivia and Marina met around Prague in places that would quickly reveal any surveillance on the young Russian. As she'd predicted, no one followed her to the nail salon, the museum café or the clothing store. Marina proved to be a canny and effective agent, securing audio of General Popov and Bogdi Król, who turned out to have a thick Agency file as a known facilitator who matched sellers and buyers of all things illegal in Eastern Europe.

And Olivia had shown up at exactly the right moment at the Prague field station seemingly custom made for the role of Marina's handler.

The audio also confirmed Marina's earlier characterization: Król courted Popov, who hadn't yet committed to selling the detonator.

"We need to move this along," said Olivia to Marina while pretending to shop for stilettos. "The audio makes it clear that this detonator is part of a package deal. Popov likely has access to weapons-grade plutonium. The reason he hasn't agreed to sell to Król's buyer is that he doesn't want it used against Assad, Russia's ally. But he's perfectly willing to sell it to the right terrorist. I need to make sure that doesn't happen."

She stopped in front of a pair of Christian Louboutin heels, her index finger tracing their black patent leather. It had been nearly four years since her first mission for the CIA in which she'd needed to get close to a wealthy, handsome financier with ties to Hamas. To catch his eye, she'd worn four-inch black-suede stilettos made by the French designer with lipstick matching their iconic red soles.

On impulse, she pushed her ankle boots and socks off as she continued speaking. "I think that next time you're in charge of procuring 'entertainment' you should introduce me to Popov."

Olivia looked up at Marina, whose large eyes conveyed both admiration and fear.

"They say bulls charge at the color red. Let's see if I can get Popov to change direction and open up to outside bids."

Olivia waited the following Saturday evening at Bar Cohiba Atmosphere for Marina and the two men, her sleek hair coiffed in a long ponytail that draped over one shoulder and a gin and rose-syrup cocktail in her hand. She'd taken a seat in the corner where she could watch the bar and the door with her back covered. Though she wore an elegant black sheath dress with a 9mm handgun in a thigh holster and a short tactical knife on the other thigh, she had no other backup. Her station chief, Henry Reardon, reluctant to assign any of the station's busy personnel to support Olivia until she had a concrete lead on the nuclear package, had sent her on her own with the words "it's something you prefer anyway, Markham."

It was the first time that Olivia had gone into the field without a support team, and the feeling of vulnerability shocked her. Sipping from the cocktail as she glanced around the small bar with leather barstools and dark-wood ceiling planks, she admitted to herself that she'd subconsciously counted on Thomas, Monica, and Bryce, whom she'd come to trust as family after a year together.

No, it was more than that.

She'd trusted Monica, who'd had her back all through her first mission, a mission that took her from the relative safety of the D.C. suburbs to the exotic and dangerous Chinese city-state of Macau. A mission that, now that she'd completed her CIA training and worked so hard to interdict actual terrorist attacks, Olivia believed should have ended her intelligence ambitions. Someone somewhere was looking out for her.

More than Monica, she'd trusted Thomas, the first man she'd been intimate with after Chase Graham, the target of that original mission. Their romance had seemed like a godsend, tailormade for two field operatives working side-by-side on the same anti-terrorism objective.

A sharp twinge caught Olivia behind her ribcage, forcing her to inhale.

She hadn't just trusted Thomas. She'd allowed herself to fall in love with him, to start thinking somewhere in the back of her mind that maybe they'd leave the CIA together in a few short years before they'd burned through the best years of their lives on a Sisyphean task. Or at the very least, transition to analyst jobs back at Langley with a home in the suburbs, two children, a minivan, and a dog.

As she played with the St. Michael medal around her neck, inconspicuous next to the glittering diamond bracelet and earrings borrowed from a local asset at Reardon's request, Olivia failed to see her target step into the club until Marina, Popov, and Król approached the bar.

Straightening, Olivia tried to get her head back in the game. It might only be a game, but it was a damn important one. Her love life or lack thereof paled in comparison.

After a few minutes, Marina swiveled in her barstool and lifted her cocktail with a slight tilt of her chin at Olivia which said, *You're up.* Then, placing a hand on Popov's shoulder, she leaned toward him to whisper into his ear.

The Russian general appraised Olivia over his shoulder as he listened. Olivia saw interest spark in his gaze. She lifted her cocktail and sipped, unable to smile in invitation and hoping that her lingering eye contact signaled the interest that she feigned.

Drink in hand, Popov moved the few meters toward her corner table.

"*Dobrý večer,*" he said in Czech. *Good evening.* Unexpectedly, he leaned forward and brushed a thumb across Olivia's cheekbone. "*Kdo ti zlomil srdce? Řekni mi to a já ho zlomím.*" *Who has broken your heart? Tell me, and I will break him.*

Startled, Olivia blinked several times as her heart picked up its pace. He'd read her too easily.

What a joke, she thought. The man willing to sell nuclear weapons to terrorists would play the chivalrous gentleman and punish the man who was unwilling to love her if it meant not stopping terrorists.

Use it against him came *Sensei* Mark's voice in her thoughts. Olivia wrapped her fingers around the St. Michael medal.

Popov's gaze followed the movement. He lifted the tiny silver disc in his large fingers and studied it.

"*Svyatoy Michael,*" he said to himself in Russian.

Thinking of *Sensei* Mark, whose voice always advised her in tough situations no matter how improbable it seemed, Olivia said in Russian, "He's the only man who has always been there for me besides my father."

Popov's eyes narrowed at her words. "Marina didn't tell me you speak Russian." He sat next to her on the other bench seat, electricity sparking between them, filled with danger rather than sexual tension. He was a large man, well over two meters tall, with a broad nose and ruddy complexion. Olivia would *not* want to find herself alone with him in a hotel room, especially if she had to disappoint his expectations for exotic sexual practices.

She shrugged a shoulder as she traced a fingertip around the top of her rose-and-gin cocktail. "Perhaps Marina didn't know. She is, after all, only a young administrative assistant." She raised her gaze and held his. "Even with training, they don't always recognize when someone approaches them for a business contact."

Olivia picked up her drink and sipped as Popov studied her, refusing to shiver at the mix of lust and suspicion in his unwavering observation.

"Even with training, I would not believe that you have anything to offer outside of your considerable charms," he said, his growling voice bringing the hairs on the back of her neck to standing. "You also can be little more than bait in a black dress."

"How about a buyer for your package who won't take it back to Syria and use it on Assad's troops?" asked Olivia, watching Popov now as a fleet gazelle watched a crouching lion. "A buyer from an African concern." She kept the details purposely vague so that she could work them out with Reardon later.

Popov said nothing for several moments. Instead, he lifted his chin at the bartender, who nodded and began making another cocktail for the Russian general. Olivia refrained from speaking and instead forced herself to remain relaxed under Popov's continued hostile glare. After a couple of minutes, the bartender personally brought Popov's drink to the table, setting it next to his elbow. Popov acknowledged its presence with a grunt, lifting and drinking it in a single large swallow before setting the empty tumbler on the table with a decisive bang.

A moment later, he gripped Olivia's wrist with viselike fingers. "Then I would say that I would like to meet this mythical buyer. But for now, I am looking for a companion for this evening, and you would suit me fine."

Olivia resisted the urge to swallow hard. It was the most dangerous moment in the evening's negotiation.

Don't back down, said *Sensei* Mark in her ear. *He's testing you, and you'll lose the hook if you agree.*

At last, Olivia shook her head, letting the slight curling of her lips suggest coyness instead of her desire to snarl. With lightning speed, she grabbed his forearm with her free hand as she rotated her hand inside his grip and pulled her hand free. Before he could react, she held Popov's wrist as she rotated his hand upward into a painful wristlock, forcing him to twist his upper body to keep from tearing ligaments and dislocating his wrist.

"I'm afraid that I'm not part of the negotiation, General Popov," she said, smiling and using his name and rank to deliver a message: *I can hurt you more than physically*. That set the hook. He'd definitely continue the negotiation, if only to try to outmaneuver her. "Marina has my contact information. I look forward to scheduling a time and place for you to meet my principal."

Then Olivia dropped Popov's hand and slid from the bench seat before grabbing her rose-and-gin cocktail and tossing the remainder back in a swift tilt of her heard. Popov had barely returned to upright when Olivia walked through the curtained entryway and out of the club—but not before noting Marina's open mouth at the bar behind her.

SIX

When Marina didn't contact her for several days, Olivia began to worry that she'd overplayed her hand or misread the situation thanks to her weird habit of hearing *Sensei* Mark's voice in her head at critical moments. Though that voice had always served her well, Olivia had every reason to believe that it came from her unwillingness to go anywhere alone with the Russian general. That and her gut reaction to his brutal grip on her wrist.

Certainly, Popov was a proud—and if she'd read his expression correctly, vindictive—man. He'd want to humiliate her as she'd humiliated him in his favorite Czech club. Olivia would have to be extremely careful during the next stages of the negotiation. And until Reardon told her whom her backup would be, she had little to do except clean her gun and spend hours in the gym in between clearing the never-ending graymail. Alone. At least she had an office in which to marinate in her own humiliation. Thomas had insisted that her move to Prague had been lateral, but Olivia knew it was a downgrade.

On the Friday after her encounter with Popov, Reardon himself knocked on Olivia's door.

"Markham, just wanted to let you know personally that Czech military intelligence has independently confirmed that Popov has been shopping around for a buyer for weapons-grade plutonium and a detonator package."

Olivia looked up from reading a letter from a man claiming to have had a long-term affair with Vladimir Putin, who'd just become president of Russia for the third time. It was a titillating idea, but the Agency knew full well that Putin had no skeletons of the sort in his closet. The letter writer promised to provide evidence, including photos and handwritten love letters, for a "minor" payout of fifty thousand euros. Olivia had long stopped wondering how to describe people who weren't crazy who nevertheless tried to con one of the most skilled espionage organizations in the world. Desperate? Naïve? Devious but not clever? All of the above?

Reardon stood just inside her doorway, a pleasant expression on his round, middle-aged analyst's face. He hadn't been in the field in a very long time or he'd know that his false congeniality was transparent.

"Czech military intelligence shared that with us?" she asked, swiveling in her seat and tilting her head.

Having been under the dominion of the Soviet Union for nearly four decades, Czechs despised Russian intelligence operations in their country. It seemed unlikely that they'd hand over information about a renegade Russian general selling nuclear material under their noses. They'd want to handle the matter in house so to speak.

Reardon shook his head in answer to her question but said nothing.

Okay then. The Agency had either wiretapped the Czechs or developed an asset among Czech military intelligence. Good to know.

"Has your asset contacted you yet?" asked Reardon. After Olivia shook her head, he said, "Then we'll go to Plan B and see if we can entice a sale. According to Czech intel, Popov has been looking around for a while and is getting a little spooked at being exposed back in Russia."

"What does that—'entice'—mean?" asked Olivia, sensing that Reardon's pleasant demeanor hid an unpleasant announcement.

"It means that I'm calling in a Special Tactical Unit with experience in buying illegal arms on the black market. They've already got a legend in place, in fact." A smug note entered Reardon's voice.

Anger and frustration burned through Olivia. He'd never intended to give her operational control or support negotiating with Popov. In fact, he was on the verge of telling her that she'd been removed from the mission that she'd been developing for months.

Olivia sat forward to argue when she glimpsed the notifications on a dating site account that she shared with Marina. A new draft message had appeared.

Marina had contacted her.

Instead of responding to Reardon, Olivia opened the draft email. It read: *Your upcoming event promises to be quite explosive. Bring a date.* A string of numbers followed.

GPS coordinates.

Olivia looked up at Reardon. "That's fabulous because I already told Popov that I'd bring my principal to meet him. The asset has just sent me the coordinates for the meeting."

She refrained from looking smug at Reardon's widened eyes at her announcement.

In the end, however, it was the team leader of the STU, a large black man with intelligent eyes, a ready smile, and an indomitable presence who told Reardon how it was going to be when Reardon tried to shut Olivia down during their mission briefing.

"Now, now," he said, his rich, jovial voice cutting across the debate between Reardon and Olivia while the rest of his team—four of the hardest-looking men that Olivia had ever seen—watched intently.

Reardon paused in the middle of speaking. Olivia, recognizing authority when confronted with it, sat back and crossed her arms over her chest. Something about Nate made her instantly trust him, though she couldn't exactly pinpoint why. Maybe it was the genuine respect that she'd seen in his gaze and the firm but not crushing grip of his hand when he'd shook hers.

Adopting the Nigerian accent of his legend, Nate said, "Isaac Abara has been known to appreciate a beautiful woman." He grinned at Olivia, who sat next to him. "And he most definitely appreciates a beautiful woman who is as smart and tough as the one he sends out to prepare the way for his negotiations. Does General Popov have a name for you?"

Olivia shook her head. "No. He simply knows me as the blonde who works for an unnamed African concern." She glanced at Reardon and back to Nate as she added, "Who rejected his advances at the club in the most humiliating way. Popov will expect to see me at your meeting. He wants payback."

Nate smiled. "I doubt that he'll achieve that with Dido, named after the indomitable queen of Carthage, and my personal facilitator."

"Didn't she commit suicide?" asked Olivia, intrigued with the proposed cover name.

"Some say she pined for Aeneas. Others think that she refused to marry a neighboring king and subjugate herself, so she took her own life," said Nate, picking up his coffee and taking a sip.

He set the cup down and continued, "Propaganda. I think anyone who managed to escape her tyrant brother—the one who murdered her husband, by the way—and found a powerful city-state in a foreign land that the upstart Rome later took three wars to subdue ... I think Dido said, 'Screw it. These men aren't worth a grain of my time or a glimpse of my beauty.' And she gathered up a few faithful servants and her most-cherished belongings and lived her life out in the desert."

Nate's admiring gaze told Olivia that he alluded to *her* with his hypothetical about the ancient queen. It was a little discomfiting coming from such an experienced Special Forces soldier, the kind who compelled everyone's attention, officers, enlisted, and civilians. Olivia almost blushed.

The next moment Reardon snorted, bringing her back to reality.

"The history lesson is all well and good," said the station chief, "but I'm not convinced Markham needs to go to Katowice with your unit."

Nate's smile disappeared. He sat back in his chair and said nothing.

His second-in-command, a ruddy-faced master sergeant named Mack, leaned toward Reardon. "It ain't up to you," he said pointedly. "Nate has operational control."

Reardon blanched at the other man's stare. And then backed down.

As it turned out, Reardon hadn't called in an STU from the CIA's Special Operations Group, or SOG. Instead, Nate and his men had been dispatched by the Joint Special Operations Command (JSOC) of the U.S. military. Nate, Mack, and the rest of the team consisting of Charles, Hector, and Bob formed an elite team from the A Squadron of the Army's 1st Special Forces Operational Detachment–Delta, otherwise known as Delta Force. The men referred to themselves as *The Unit* or *D-Boys*.

And Nate, a sergeant major with more than two decades in Special Forces, wanted Olivia on the mission. Reardon had done everything he could to prevent that, from mischaracterizing his own role in the team's presence to trying to minimize Olivia's involvement even before the mission briefing.

That certainly put Nate's allusion to Dido's fate in a whole new light.

After Mack's pointed assertion, Reardon said nothing more while the D-Boys and Olivia discussed the logistics for meeting with Popov. Marina had sent GPS coordinates for a dive bar in Katowice, Poland, whose owner, Kacper Bryk, smuggled drugs and guns for Eastern European crime syndicates. Bogdi Król, not wanting to lose a sale, had clearly reached out to a colleague for help finding other potential buyers.

Popov, smelling a payday, had decided to make the most money he could by letting Olivia's principal bid on the nuclear package.

That meant an auction for a weapon of mass destruction. An auction they could not lose.

The team and Olivia arrived in Katowice later that day after an easy four-hour drive east from Prague in a nondescript service van. Though the men had clearly been up for some time, they settled for napping to get them through reconnaissance of Kacper Bryk's bar, The Wild Stallion. In fact, they wouldn't sleep until they'd set up a field command center and a surveillance perimeter. And then they'd sleep in rotating shifts until the mission moved to direct action when nobody slept.

Olivia, who'd been too wired to doze, watched the battle-hardened soldiers with some envy as they leaned against the sides of the van with their arms crossed. She'd gotten out of the rhythm of the field in the past four months. She hoped her eagerness and inexperience didn't prove a stumbling block for them. She wanted to prove to Nate that he hadn't misjudged her.

Katowice, the capital of the Silesia province in southwestern Poland, had recently reformed Mariacka Street, the three-block main street lined with bars and strip clubs where The Wild Stallion, a featureless brick building, loomed not far from St. Mary's Cathedral on the eastern end.

Bob and Mack each found separate buildings from which to establish overwatch of The Wild Stallion, while Charles, the demolitions expert, and Hector, the team medic, stayed at street level in positions with line-of-sight on the bar's front and rear entrances.

Olivia and Nate, scheduled to meet with Bryk at nine that evening, went to rest in a local hotel. Nate, pulling his duffel from the van after handing Olivia hers, said casually, "Nothing dulls the reflexes and the thought processes like lack of sleep." He turned to her with a serious expression. "Get some shuteye, soldier. I need all my weapons sharp, especially the tip of the spear. You hear me?"

Olivia blinked several times, taken aback. Nate, not waiting to hear her response, turned and went into the hotel. Strangely, Nate's words had the desired effect. Once in her room, Olivia dropped her bag on the floor and lay down, falling asleep almost as soon as her head hit the pillow. She woke with a start, immediately checking her watch. 6 p.m. She had plenty of time to shower, dress, and meet Nate for a quick meal before going to The Wild Stallion.

Nate said nothing, his wide, white grin splitting his face, when Olivia joined him an hour later. She'd chosen to dress in an expensive tailored suit, one she'd long ago added to her wardrobe to signal a certain level of professionalism and refinement. It also allowed her to hide all sorts of weapons, from the deadly tactical pen in an inside jacket pocket to the concealed Kel-Tec P11 micro 9mm at the back of her waist and a second in her ankle boot. Apparently, Isaac Abara approved of his assistant's clothing choices.

They ate quickly, reviewing pictures of the interior of the bar supplied by a local asset, as well as the surveillance photos of Bryk's known associates, including a particularly thuggish man named Jerzego Miazga, who acted as Bryk's bartender and hitman.

They were met outside the hotel by Charles, wearing a slick gray suit with a black shirt and dark sunglasses even though it was evening, who acted as their driver for this mission. The military-grade armored Mercedes G500 had tinted windows and ballistic glass that could withstand everything up to a 50-caliber sniper round. Isaac Abara not only had money, he wanted everyone to notice the beefy SUV and assume his driver was locked and loaded. Which he was.

At The Wild Stallion, a tall, slender woman with a snapping black gaze and a graceful strut guided them to a corner booth. Both Olivia and Nate studied their surroundings, she overtly and he surreptitiously. Olivia thanked God that she had such a cool customer leading the mission. Behind his joking and grinning, the team leader's gaze constantly evaluated the bar around them for threats and opportunities.

Olivia used slightly different parameters.

She'd noted the reference to sex trafficking in Bryk's Agency file, and now everything filtered through that piece of information. The women in the seedy Polish bar displayed the defeated and timid visages of prostitutes in the iron grip of their pimp. Several reminded her of Anja, the German woman she'd been compelled to save at the Berlin Christmas Market. Some even sported bruises on faces and arms, though to be fair, Olivia actually cared to look under their makeup.

Johns and buyers didn't care.

Their server drew Olivia's attention among these beaten-down women. She had unusual dark-gray eyes fringed with thick, dark lashes. Her glossy black hair fell in luxurious curls to her shoulders. When she delivered Olivia and Nate's drinks, bruises peeked from beneath the fabric of her long sleeves. Despite this, her prowl suggested more predator than prey.

Interesting.

Across from them, Miazga, a tall man with the physique of a laborer, all broad shoulders and massive biceps, dumped ice into a bin behind the bar, a cigarette dangling from the corner of his mouth. A man of average height, his dirty blond hair slipping across his forehead, spoke to their server as she approached the bar.

Olivia read disgust in the tilt of the woman's head as she looked over her shoulder at the new man. As he flinched in response, light from the kitchen illuminated his face when the swinging door behind them opened.

Kacper Bryk.

Curious. This whiplike server, who could have dominated runways in Paris and Milan, frightened Bryk.

A moment later, Bryk approached, lighting a cigarette as he walked. He stopped next to their table as he clicked the lighter closed, blowing smoke into the air adjacent at the same time. He studied them for a long moment until the server, whom Olivia had continued to watch, brought them small liqueur glasses filled with a honey-colored liquid.

Bryk gestured toward the liqueur. "*Krupnik*. My family recipe. Let us toast our partnership."

The enigmatic server's gaze flickered. She said nothing but turned away.

Olivia narrowed her eyes, considering the other woman's reaction. She ignored the glass in front of her. Nate didn't even look at the *krupnik*.

Instead, he addressed their host. "Mr. Bryk, I have traveled a long way. Let us dispense with these niceties and talk business."

Bryk ignored Nate to stare at Olivia. "How much for the blonde?"

"She is not for sale," said Nate, an edge in his words. "I am here for the package. Name your price, and I will pay it."

Bryk turned back. He lifted his own drink and sipped, studying them through heavy lids as smoke from his lit cigarette curled around his face. A creeping sensation brought bile to Olivia's throat.

"There are other interested parties, Mr. Abara. Very interested. I will hear your offer and consider it. But for now, enjoy the entertainment my club has to offer. I promise you will never have better for free."

After removing her short white apron, their server moved toward the mic in the corner of the bar. Though she wore jeans and a black, long-sleeved T-shirt with the faded logo of a Polish vodka brand on the back, she looked comfortable with everyone's gazes now on her.

And when she began singing the 80s-era Madonna song *Live to Tell*, her husky mezzo-soprano voice and a delivery reminiscent of a power metal singer held her audience in thrall, including Olivia.

Wow.

This woman appeared to be the same age as Olivia. She couldn't have heard this song when it came out. Yet her performance made it her personal anthem.

The server's gaze connected with Olivia's. A current of recognition passed between them.

After the set ended, Olivia excused herself and followed the woman into The Wild Stallion's dirty restroom while Nate spoke with Bryk at their table. Though the woman didn't look surprised to see her, she still watched Olivia with the wariness of a trapped wild animal.

Without stopping to consider what she did, Olivia laid a hand on the woman's arm and asked in Czech, *"Jste zde ze své svobodné vůle?" Are you here of your free will? Mohu pomoci tobě i ostatním ženám. I can help you and the other women.*

A startled look flitted over the server's face before she clamped her features shut. She ignored Olivia and brushed past her to leave.

Olivia let her go and returned to Nate and the negotiation with Bryk, whose sleepy gaze followed her through the bar. The two silent men smoked Cubanos. Though Nate still wore a genial expression, hard lines radiated from the corners of his eyes. The untouched *krupnik* glasses remained on the table among empty glasses and a full ashtray.

It wasn't going well.

Bryk pulled his cigar from his mouth and dropped its burning tip into a half-filled pint glass. He checked his watch. "Negotiations close in five minutes, Mr. Abara. Have you given me your final offer?"

All at once Olivia understood what the true negotiation was. Bryk wanted her, likely for Popov, though the way his gaze devoured her, he would sample the goods first himself. Why hadn't she seen it before?

She could be bait. And leverage her position to help the women here, if she was right about them being part of the package.

Negotiations close in five minutes.

Glancing around, Olivia noticed that most of the trafficked women had disappeared. Time to move this along. She'd find a way somehow to keep those women from disappearing with Popov.

Olivia telegraphed her intentions by sauntering up to the table and lifting one of the glasses of *krupnik* before draining it. Swiping the back of her hand across her lips, she set the empty liqueur glass upside down on the tabletop.

"Negotiations are over," she said, ignoring Nate, whose heated glare seared the side of her face. "Tell Popov he's got a deal."

Bryk grinned. He lifted his chin toward Miazga, who nodded and began to come out from behind the bar.

Nate rose partway out of his seat and said in his Isaac Abara accent, "Now hold on. Nothing happens until I examine the package."

"And I'm telling you that the package is off the table until this one"—Bryk lifted his chin toward Olivia—"satisfies Popov's demands. It's his condition, my friend."

Nate snarled, his hand going to the weapon holstered inside his jacket as he stood to his full six-foot-four imposing height. "And my condition is that she is not for sale."

A moment later, Charles, his weapon visible in a two-handed grip, burst into The Wild Stallion and raced toward Nate and Olivia.

"Boss, time to go. We've locked down the package's position."

"Dido, with me!" Nate's voice boomed across the bar as he pivoted toward the hard-eyed sergeant, who'd already pulled up short and surveyed the bar around them.

All hell broke loose almost simultaneously.

Dizziness flooded Olivia, causing her to stumble into the table next to her. She threw out her hand, missed the table's edge, and fell to one knee. Sharp pain and nausea threatened to overwhelm her.

The *krupnik*. It had been laced with something.

Olivia tried to rise to follow the two D-Boys until she felt an iron grip on her upper arm. The next instant, she'd been pulled back against Miazga. She started to resist when Bryk tapped her cheek with the tip of a wicked-looking knife.

"Dido, with me," he said, mimicking Nate's words in eerie imitation of the Isaac Abara voice.

The bar swirled into an oily mess of dark wood, dim lights, cheap furniture, and scurrying patrons as Miazga dragged Olivia away from her teammates.

SEVEN

H ands shook Olivia awake none too gently. She woke with her cheek pressed against dirty metal, a blinding headache making her eye sockets hurt.

"*Kdyby hloupost nadnášela, tak se tady budete vznášet jako holubička.*" *If stupidity floats, you will float here like a dove,* said a woman in Czech.

The server from The Wild Stallion.

"Better free my hands and feet then before I bump into the ceiling," said Olivia in Czech, her voice hoarse.

The woman sniffed and moved away. But a moment later, Olivia felt a blade catch on the zip ties around her wrists before they snapped. The woman helped her to sit upright before turning to free Olivia's ankles.

Olivia, wincing as she rubbed her wrists, looked around them. They rode in the back of an unconditioned panel truck. Silent women, mostly teenagers lured by Bryk with promises of modeling jobs, slumped against the sides of the truck, either watching them with disinterest or gazing into an imaginary distance. Sour sweat and sharp fear mixed in a suffocating miasma around them. Olivia's nose wrinkled against her will.

The women that Bryk trafficked.

Olivia looked back at the woman who'd freed her. Despite the sweat slicking her skin, she exuded a coolness that Olivia admired. The dark-haired server sat on her heels studying Olivia with a glittering, impenetrable gaze.

"Though perhaps I deserve your scorn. I was trying to rescue these women, not join their ranks. But something tells me you"—she lifted her chin toward the server before continuing—"don't need rescuing. You look like a model, but you move like someone trained to fight. Czech military?"

The woman scowled and refused to answer. Instead, she appeared to listen as the truck ground to a halt. Then she made her way to the rear of the truck through the passive women, gripped the short rope on the lift gate, and tugged. The gate rose a meter.

It hadn't even been locked.

The woman, whom Olivia was more certain than ever was an embedded Czech military intelligence officer, dropped to the ground and disappeared.

Well. That was friendly.

Olivia began urging the women in Ukrainian and Russian to follow her as she maneuvered through them to the rear. She jumped down and swiveled to see that not a single woman had moved. If anything, some of them had shrunk farther into the recesses of the box truck.

A warning shout from the trees on the other side of the road drew Olivia's gaze.

Just as something hammered the side of her head, sending her to her knees.

Eyes watering and nausea pouring up her throat, Olivia fought a massive wave of dizziness that threatened to swamp her in a kaleidoscope of unreal sensory input.

Hissing echoed around her before a dark fury erupted from the woods even as other men rushed from the road bracketing the stopped truck.

Olivia's jaw dropped.

The Czech officer bent and scooped a handful of dirt from the side of the road, flinging it at the gun-wielding man looming over Olivia. He hesitated as the gritty soil blinded him.

The Czech didn't.

She ripped the long-barreled weapon from his hands, swinging its stock into his head in a quick, smooth movement. Even as he dropped like a sack of bones, she flipped the stock into her hands and shot another man who appeared at the corner of the truck. Then turned and shot a third man from the other side.

The tactical rifle looked like an extension of her arms.

Olivia didn't have any more time to admire the graceful economy of her companion's fighting style. Other men sprinted toward them from the road behind the truck.

She scrambled for the gun dropped by the man next to her. The next seconds passed in a blur in which Olivia reacted largely by instinct and muscle memory. Somewhere during the initial moments after she'd shot a man who'd stopped a short distance away to aim his weapon and then shot the man next to him, she'd gotten to her feet and pulled the Czech into the woods.

Without taking her gaze from the road, the Czech, who'd covered their retreat with a continuous bullet spray, said, "Nice to see that you are not completely incompetent. I was beginning to wonder about the CIA." She said this in perfect English. "Now we will see if your partner can follow directions."

Before Olivia could ask what that meant, Nate's voice came from behind them. "I resent the suggestion. Who do you think staged this little ambush?"

Olivia started. She hadn't seen or heard the team leader's approach. Looking over her shoulder, she saw him, flamboyant still in his Isaac Abara suit but wearing a hard expression as he trained his gaze on the road beyond them.

The Czech didn't look back at Nate. Instead, she raised her weapon and fired at something unseen. A grunt followed by a thud told the story of what.

She glanced at Nate, her narrow gaze cool and unfathomable. "Does that mean you did not secure the package?"

"My team is handling it," said Nate, his lips compressed. "This little distraction is simply that: a distraction."

The Czech grunted and kept her head on a swivel, constantly scanning the perimeter demarcated by the road and surrounding trees. She sniffed. "I should hope so. If Bryk figures out that I am the one who alerted the Americans to his little deal, my own mission will be compromised."

Olivia, who'd remained silent while the other two spoke, asked as she lifted her chin toward the truck, "What about the women?"

"What about them?" asked the Czech officer without looking at Olivia. "Time to go," she added, "before Bryk sends some men to investigate."

Without waiting for a response, the other woman, the tactical rifle aimed and ready, began jogging toward the rear of the truck and the abandoned rear escort vehicle.

Olivia turned toward the truck. She *couldn't* just leave the sex victims sitting there, stunned and helpless. Maybe she could drive them somewhere safe....

Before she could take a step, Nate's massive hand clamped onto her upper arm. "Let it go, Markham. That's a direct order, in case you've forgotten who's in charge here. I read your Agency file. I know you've been having a little trouble staying focused. It's why I decided to use you as bait with Bryk and Popov. Still, I would have preferred not having to extract you from a delivery of sex slaves for a Kosovar terrorist."

Olivia's eyes widened. Her brain refused to comprehend what Nate had just told her: that he'd used her to distract Bryk while the rest of the team searched for the nuclear detonator and weapons-grade plutonium.

While she gaped, Nate tugged her, stumbling, behind him as he walked toward the vehicle now idling behind the truck with the Czech officer at the wheel.

Panic gripped Olivia. She planted her feet, the image of the women filling her imagination. Her St. Michael medal scorched her skin. When Nate, swearing softly, pivoted to pull her with him, Olivia stepped forward and slipped her free arm under his. Then she twisted as she grabbed his upper arm, throwing him over her shoulder.

He landed on the ground with a thud.

Chest heaving at the exertion, Olivia said, "We can't just leave them here!"

And then Nate had rolled and come to his feet in a liquid motion that really took her breath away. Anger had wiped all the good humor from his features. Briefly, Olivia wondered if she'd gone too far.

"I don't want to 'just leave them here,'" said the big Spec-Ops soldier through a clenched jaw, "but rescuing one woman is all I've got time for on my agenda today."

Olivia blinked at that. *She* didn't need saving.

The next instant, an unseen shooter tagged Nate, whose large frame wavered as he absorbed a bullet to the upper back.

The Czech officer popped out of the driver's side of the commandeered SUV, firing over the hood toward the shooter hidden in the woods beyond them.

"The Kosovar," she said as Olivia lunged to put a shoulder under Nate's armpit, taking some of his weight as they staggered to the rear passenger door. "He sent a team to take delivery."

Nate managed to open the door and fall-slide into the backseat. Olivia ducked in beside him, ignoring the bright blood slicking the black leather.

"Go, go, go!" yelled Olivia.

The Czech responded by backing the SUV one-handed as she continued firing through the open passenger window. Bullets whined and ricocheted from the vehicle's armored metal. And then, the attack ended almost as soon as it had started.

Olivia saw black-clad, armed men rushing to the truck where the women remained, their pale, unmoving forms still visible.

She'd failed to lead them to safety and freedom.

She'd gotten her team leader wounded.

She may have risked an ally's cover.

Turning, she saw Nate slouched in the seat corner, a hand pressed against the exit wound on his shoulder and watching her.

"I'm sorry," she said.

Nate shook his head. "Me, too, Dido. Me, too."

The next hours passed in a blur for Olivia. While Nate had headed off alone to rescue his renegade CIA adjunct, the rest of the D-Boys had recovered the nuclear detonator and plutonium before it could be secured by an ethnic Serb from Kosovo who disagreed with international efforts to normalize relations with the nascent Kosovar government.

Bryk had, indeed, found a more suitable purchaser for Popov's illicit nuclear material. That's because Mother Russia backed Serbia's declaration that the new Republic of Kosovo had been formed illegally. Selling arms to a Serb could almost be seen as patriotic, if self-serving.

As a result of Nate's decision to extract Olivia, the D-Boys had been forced to leave Poland without their injured leader. He and Olivia were on their own.

Bryk and the Kosovar terrorist, likely together, would be looking for them. Especially when the Kosovar learned that his people had seriously wounded Nate. Only Popov had left the scene a happier, *wealthier* man.

They'd stopped to tend Nate's shoulder once they'd gotten clear of the ambush. The Czech officer, a captain named Alžběta Czerná, had navigated via back roads to the suburbs of Żory, a small city not far from the Czech border. Now they were parked at the back of a busy sports club where their stolen SUV would draw no casual attention.

"I know someone who can get you two into Germany," said Captain Czerná. "You should be able to get medical help at one of the American military bases."

"Good," said Nate on a groan. The indomitable Unit leader had lost a lot of blood while they escaped, and his gray-tinged, compressed lips conveyed a world of pain that his silence during the drive had only underscored. "But Markham and I need to split up. With luck, the Kosovar's men will follow my trail. Can you get her past Bryk's men? She's expected back in Prague anyway."

"Wait! No, Nate! You need help getting to Germany. Let me go with you!" said Olivia, shocked that the older operative would suggest going on without her.

If she understood Nate at all—and she would bet her life on it—he would sacrifice himself to give her a better shot at escaping.

Well, not on her watch.

The Czech officer studied Olivia. "You are both right," she said, turning to Nate. "This one"—here she jerked her chin toward Olivia—"would never make it back to Czechia on her own." She paused and narrowed her eyes at Nate. "Yet your injury is too grave for you to travel alone to Germany."

Olivia tried not to bristle at the other woman's assessment. Given how the operation had turned out, it was more than fair. But she was more concerned about Nate than herself.

Leaning against the SUV, she folded her arms and asked the other woman, "Do you have something better in mind?"

Captain Czerná shrugged. "You would probably not like it."

"Try me."

"Whoa," said Nate, exhaling heavily. "I may be two quarts low, but I'm still conscious and in charge."

Olivia looked at him, her expression softening as she took in the sweat glazing his temples and the way he listed against the side of the vehicle.

"I think we're a little outside the playbook, Sergeant Major. Besides, the captain here outranks you." She smiled to take the sting from her observation. She turned back to the other woman. "You have something in mind related to your position with Bryk? Which is what, by the way?"

Captain Czerná held Olivia's gaze with her dark, unfathomable one. "I got into Bryk's operation as one of his 'girls,'" she said, spitting the word. "He likes to sample the goods. Unfortunately for him, I taste bad. As a result, he made me their caretaker."

From what little she'd seen of the Czech officer, the only way *that* play would work with Bryk was if the Polish crime lord believed he held something over the prickly woman.

A flash of intuition told Olivia what.

"You promised to make sure they did as they were told as long as Bryk didn't beat them," she said. "He allowed it because he thought it gave him more control over you." She cocked her head and pressed her lips together thinking. "You also agreed to sing in the club."

Captain Czerná nodded but said nothing.

"He doesn't know you were on that truck," said Olivia, concluding her guesswork.

Captain Czerná shook her head. "You are not as stupid as you seem."

Olivia, who knew the Czech's bluntness wasn't personal, said wryly, "Thanks."

The other woman went on as if Olivia hadn't spoken. "You just have a soft heart. It will get you killed someday."

"But not today," said Olivia. She looked over at Nate, who'd closed his eyes and breathed shallowly while listening to them speak. "Today I'm listening to whatever idea you have in mind for getting my team leader to safety."

Captain Czerná, who'd been scanning their environment for threats as soon as they'd stabilized Nate's wound, nodded again.

"We will use him as—how do you say?"—here she snapped her fingers as impatience flitted across her features—"chum."

Olivia winced at the image of bloody bait fish thrown behind boats to attract larger fish, including sharks.

"It's what I was going to do anyway," said Nate, exhaling on a soft grunt.

"Yes, but in this scenario, we will be prepared to dynamite whatever swims into range," said Captain Czerná.

"You don't strike me as someone who wastes time with a rod and reel," said Olivia drily.

The other woman looked at her and sniffed. "Not on bottom feeders like Bryk."

"I like her," said Nate. A smile ghosted his face.

A doubt niggled Olivia. She'd already exposed them and nearly gotten Nate killed. She asked the captain, "What about your mission?"

"Let me worry about that," said Captain Czerná, heading toward the SUV's cargo hold.

Olivia persisted. "Won't you be compromised with Bryk?"

This time when the beautiful but enigmatic Czech looked back at her, something alien and indomitable peeked out. A shiver rolled down Olivia's spine. She gripped her St. Michael medal for comfort, something she hadn't done in a long time.

"If we do this right, he will never know that it was me."

That meant no survivors.

"I like her," said Nate again. This time, his face had hardened. He even stood taller as if he'd gotten a second wind. Likely it was adrenaline surging at the prospect of a battle.

Somehow Captain Czerná had succeeded in stanching the bullet wound, which she'd declared a through-and-through, missing major arteries *and* the shoulder joint. She'd even fashioned a very serviceable field sling to immobilize his arm. Even so, they needed to get Nate to skilled medical care where antibiotics and painkillers awaited him.

They spent the next few minutes planning tactics, which involved Captain Czerná muttering as she rummaged through the SUV for anything useful.

"Who has Semtex but no detonator?" she asked without turning around.

"No burner phone?" asked Olivia, wishing she could step in and examine the cache.

But the Czech officer had asserted herself at Nate's tacit approval of her plan, and Olivia had opted to take watch over their surroundings. It also allowed her to observe Nate surreptitiously. So far, he was holding his own.

When Captain Czerná didn't answer, Olivia, impatient, asked, "How about a machine gun? You can use a tracer round."

The other woman looked back at her. "I have something better." She held up a pineapple-shaped object.

"A Mk II," said Nate. "Where the hell'd they get *that* relic?"

"It makes no matter," said Captain Czerná, a wicked grin transforming her normally severe features, "because I have the perfect use for it, along with a rubber band."

All that remained was for Nate to play the part of wounded prey.

Bryk, like the proverbial spider, had a web of connections leading from his base in Katowice. Żory, only 40 kilometers southwest, lay on the route to Ostrava in the Czech Republic. It was the obvious destination for anyone fleeing an arms deal gone bad. They'd just need to give Bryk a little targeting information.

Captain Czerná picked the site for their Trojan Horse. "Mszana, twenty minutes from here."

Nate's wide grin showed Olivia that he knew the Polish village. "Seems appropriate for using a World-War-II-era grenade to ambush the bad guys," he said.

"Are you up to driving?" asked Olivia, unable to keep concern from her voice.

Nate's gaze sparked. "Sister, I was born ready."

"Okay, then," said Olivia. "Let's do this."

Olivia and Captain Czerná approached a young couple leaving the club. As Olivia asked in halting Polish for directions to the border crossing, the captain lifted a cellphone from the unsuspecting male's bag, which she'd use to call Miazga, Bryk's hitman, when the time was right. Then the Czech officer hotwired a car while Olivia and Nate transferred weapons from the SUV to its trunk. Afterwards, the two Americans departed, Captain Czerná trailing them until they left Żory.

They picked up a tail on the A1 outside of Świerklany Górne, two armored Mercedes AMG SUVs that raced toward them like a matched pair of black predators.

Nate punched the gas. Their armored vehicle lurched forward, weaving in the light traffic as he simulated an out-of-control and desperate driver, which, given how crazy the Czech's plan was, wasn't far from the truth. The AMGs followed nimbly, closing the distance as shooters leaned out of the front passenger windows and fired at them. A shot connected with a rear tire on their SUV. It bucked like a wild bronco, yanking them into the next lane and forcing one AMG to fall back or be run off the road.

Nate white-knuckled their vehicle as the run-flat tire allowed him to maintain highway speed. At the last moment, he swerved onto the ramp leading west off the highway. The AMGs shot past the exit, their engines roaring.

Two minutes later, Nate took a hard left towards Mszana. For the moment at least they'd shaken the hunters off.

"There!" said Olivia, pointing toward a section of the road bordered by cultivated fields.

The SUV raced to the spot before Nate slammed on the brakes and slumped over the steering wheel, his breathing ragged and his forehead shiny. Fresh blood soaked the sling.

He'd clearly reached the end of his limits.

Eight

Lying on her stomach among a stand of trees with a Vzor 58 assault rifle next to her, Captain Alžběta Czerná watched the road toward Mszana. Farther south where the road intersected with the main street, a column of thick gray smoke spiraled to the clear blue sky.

It wasn't the best hide or ambush site, but she'd had to make do with the realities of the location. Even so, she'd minimized exposure and unnecessary casualties by warning civilians off. After placing a few well-aimed shots when local traffic approached, she'd torched the stolen car and left it to block the entrance to this road only minutes before. It was unlikely that Bryk's men would use the local route but not impossible. The burning car would at least give them pause. It would also alert them that the Americans had support.

Where *were* the Americans? Without their SUV as a Trojan Horse, the whole plan fell apart.

She shrugged. She had the option to burn her cover with Jerzego—and then shoot as many of the Polish bastards as she could.

But she'd rather do it knowing that the Americans had made it into Czechia and weren't a smoldering wreck on the A1.

She glanced down at the assault rifle, her lips pulling back from her teeth. A Czech Army rifle, the VZ 58 had been a staple weapon for the past 50 years, until last year when the army had finally moved to the CZ 805 Bren. It was clear where some of the old stock had ended up. Hence her mission to embed with Bryk's organization and discover who from the army had been selling him weapons.

Twisting her wrist, Beta checked her watch. She didn't really need to consult a timepiece. Her internal clock was highly accurate. As long as her new teammates stuck to the plan, her impromptu exfil would enable their escape *and* remove a thorn in her side. She'd be able to return to The Wild Stallion without the brutish Jerzego staring at her as if she were a particularly succulent bit of roast meat. She wasn't afraid of him—he was too stupid to realize that she was a bigger predator than he was—but she didn't need the messiness so close to Bryk.

Engine sounds alerted her to the approach of a vehicle.

Bending her eye to the VZ 58's sight, she watched as the armored vehicle that she and the Americans had escaped in earlier that morning careened into place, the heavy chassis rocking as the driver smashed the brakes.

Through the glass, Beta saw the big American soldier leaning against the windshield.

Hovna. Would he be able to get clear of the SUV before Jerzego's pack arrived?

Beta clenched her jaw.

If they were anywhere in the open, it was unlikely that the Poles would bother capturing the American Spec Ops soldier. As for the beautiful blonde ...

From nowhere, a massive male strode toward the idling SUV. Beta looked away from the assault rifle and shook her head, blinking, before bringing her gaze back.

Where the hell did *he* come from? Had she failed to keep her situational awareness intact?

No, she would swear she hadn't let her guard down. In fact, she had an uncanny ability to sense incursions when in the field.

The civilian reached the Americans and opened the driver's door. Then he pulled the soldier free and slung his unconscious form over his shoulder like a sack of wheat.

Despite his burden and the obvious gunshot wound on the other man, the stranger radiated an air of purposeful menace. Something about the way the sunlight outlined his figure sent shivers down Beta's spine.

A moment later, the female American spy—'Olivia,' she'd called herself when she insisted on thanking Beta—jumped out of the SUV, slammed the door, and ran around to the side with the gas tank. She reappeared at the back of the vehicle and glanced toward Beta's hiding spot before flashing a thumbs up.

The clock was ticking. If Beta's estimate held—and she was betting lives that it would—the hunters she'd sicced on the Americans would arrive before it ran out.

Olivia disappeared again, this time to enact her part from the field on the other side of the road where Beta had dropped a CZ Scorpion EVO 3—a Czech carbine rifle—along with a Glock, and a bag of 9mm cartridges that both weapons chambered.

Beta, who'd been consumed by this scene in her staged drama, whipped her gaze back toward the two males. They needed to take cover *immediately*.

The Viking headed across the field toward the trees where Beta hid. He stared straight at her. In the near distance, the distinct engine sounds of AMG SUVs growled.

"Hide, you fool!" she muttered, "Or they will pick the pieces of your carcass off the pavement five minutes from now."

The Viking's upper lip curled as if he heard her, and then he began sprinting with the American. The trees had swallowed them when several black AMGs appeared. Beta glimpsed Jerzego's mousy hair and heavy jaw in the lead SUV. The hitman threw up a hand to halt the caravan twenty meters from the abandoned vehicle.

"Come closer, my dear," she murmured, lowering her eye to the rifle's sight.

More vehicles arrived from the south and encircled the still-idling SUV. Armed men poured onto the road, some taking up position behind open doors and hoods.

Fantastický. The Kosovar's men had joined Bryk's. She hoped that the terrorist leader himself numbered among them.

Beta whispered, "Closer," and refrained from looking at her watch. She didn't have time to find her aim again.

Jerzego motioned for some of the men to come with him. Together, they approached the empty vehicle, their weapons trained and ready.

And then the rubber band depressing the grenade's lever finished dissolving in the gasoline in the armored vehicle's tank.

1,500 kilograms of red-hot shrapnel blasted across a radius of a hundred meters and a couple of dozen vulnerable armed men.

After the concussive force dissipated, it was simple enough for Beta and Olivia to dispatch anyone still standing.

Reardon himself met Olivia and Nate with an Agency STU at the Czech border. Nate, who'd roused as they crossed through border control long enough to see Captain Czerná conferring with one of the guards, had lost consciousness again before Olivia's boss and his team arrived. Mack and Hector, the Unit's medic, joined them in Ostrava, where they moved Nate to a large sedan with smoked-glass windows and sped away before Olivia could tell them how sorry she was.

After the debriefing at the Prague station, Olivia requested, and was granted, a three-day leave. She had something she had to do, and the Company wouldn't approve. Reardon's cold expression and flat lips as he listened to Olivia's account sent misgiving through her. The man didn't like her, that was clear. If he discovered what she planned to do with her time off, he'd use it against her.

Olivia had never felt so alone. She didn't even know if what she had to do was the right thing or just some unhealthy obsession stemming from her cousin's murder.

It was the exact compulsion that had prompted her to stand up to the terrorists in Ibiza three years ago—the response that got her noticed by the CIA in the first place. Ever since she'd crossed the border into the Czech Republic, she'd been haunted with the sense that she'd left something undone. Something that gripped her and wouldn't let go.

The sudden appearance of the gigantic stranger in Mszana who'd carried Nate to safety played over and over in Olivia's thoughts. It had been an answer to a prayer she hadn't consciously made, so she'd accepted it. But what did it mean that she'd thought it was *Sensei* Mark at first? Just like on the Breitscheidplatz in Berlin ...

Uneasiness filled Olivia. She toyed with the St. Michael pendant that her mentor had given her to wear during her darkest days after Emily's murderer's trial. It always seemed to warm when she needed a reminder of his steadfast presence.

Never forget who you are or what your true mission is. When in doubt, listen to your conscience and think of me, he'd said that last time she'd seen him on Cape Cod three years ago—before she'd finished getting her intelligence degree and committed to a career with the Central Intelligence Agency.

What *was* her true mission? She'd stopped even wondering what he'd meant by that and just focused on accomplishing the objectives that the Company gave her.

Now, the unnerving feeling that her mentor walked at her side, both silently supportive and disappointed in her at the same time, sent Olivia to get her go bag, grab the Company-issued Polish passport, and make her way across the border back into Poland on an unsanctioned mission. She had to find the trafficked women that Bryk had traded to the Kosovar terrorist, the ones she'd been forced to leave behind when she and Nate escaped.

And she knew exactly who to approach for help.

When Olivia found Captain Czerná, the Czech officer had backed a man against the wall of the alley behind The Wild Stallion, a hawk-billed karambit under his jaw and a forearm pressed into his chest. She didn't turn as Olivia neared, not bothering to hide the sound of her steps.

"Why are you here?" asked Beta instead. It was more of a growl than a question.

"You know why," said Olivia, her arms folded. "The women. I'm pretty sure that's why you're interrogating this guy. Am I right?"

That got Beta's attention.

She swiped the karambit across the terrified man's cheek, the deft stroke slicing a hairline so fine his skin didn't know it needed to bleed for a whole second.

"He told me what I needed to know. I simply reminded him that Bryk does not like to get his hands dirty. I, however, do what needs doing."

Olivia dipped her chin when the other woman gazed at her. "As do I."

Beta spit on the pavement next to the man's shoes. He turned and ran.

She turned to face Olivia, sliding the karambit closed with a soft *snick*. For a moment, her dark expression and the cloying scent of smoke in the close quarters called up the image of something demonic.

Olivia refrained from touching her St. Michael pendant. It was becoming a little too reflexive.

The other woman narrowed her eyes and studied Olivia. Then she nodded. "Bryk has them in an apartment building he owns in Chorzów."

Olivia tilted her head. "Would you like help recovering them?"

Beta tossed something at her. Without thinking, Olivia caught it. The hawk-billed karambit.

"Can you use that?"

Olivia opened and closed the tactical knife one-handed, transferring it between hands, before offering it back.

Beta, watching her, shook her head. "Keep it. Harder to trace than bullets. And more satisfying."

Olivia nodded and slipped the wicked little knife into her pants pocket. "I'll take that as yes."

On the way out of the city, they stopped at one of Beta's storage units where the Czech captain grabbed a black military duffel heavy with weapons.

Then Olivia drove them to Chorzów, a city less than ten kilometers north of Katowice. Although it had only half a million residents, Chorzów was situated in the Silesian metro area. The entire conurbation—the technical term for a region where individual municipalities spread into a dense urban amoeba—had a population of nearly six million.

Unfortunately for those six million residents, criminals didn't confine their activity to one jurisdiction. And the disparate law enforcement authorities didn't always play nice with each other. Bryk, like any good CEO or terrorist leader, had compartmentalized and distributed his diverse enterprises so that if one site got raided, his business survived. In the past eight months, he'd taken over a Czech rival's operation in Ostrava, making his own even more resilient.

Or so he believed.

As it happened, Beta had spent the past six months mapping Bryk's organization. She knew to a fine degree what resources, including people, and what sites he controlled.

The two-bedroom apartment in Chorzów where Bryk's men held the nine women sat east of Stadion Ruchu, not far from the train tracks. Olivia and Beta parked nearby where they could scout the surrounding blocks before returning to a café across the street for tactical planning.

It wasn't going to be easy getting the women out.

First, Bryk had all of his operations monitored remotely in Katowice, so reinforcements would be dispatched as soon as they breached the front door.

Second, the fourth-floor apartment had only one entry point and a trio of armed guards.

Third, they had to assume that some of the women were in bad shape, either wounded or, more likely, ill from lack of food and poor conditions.

Fourth, Bryk had police sources who would tip him off about an imminent raid.

But none of these were insurmountable.

Beta, her arms folded and an untouched coffee on the table in front of her, watched the street outside the café window with a scowl twisting her fine features. "The men Bryk uses to guard the women *mají hlavy kysaného zelí.*"

"'Have sauerkraut heads'?" asked Olivia. "I've never heard that Czech idiom."

"That is because I just coined it," said Beta. She picked up her coffee and sipped, making a face.

Olivia, who'd observed that the Czech preferred the beverage scalding, guessed that it had cooled too much.

Then Beta turned her dark gaze on Olivia, who sensed banked fury behind it. "How else do you explain their primary responsibility is to watch soccer games on TV and eat takeout *pierogi*? Bryk could leave the door open. Those women will not try to escape."

A faint acrid whiff of smoke tickled Olivia's nostrils. She ignored it. In the short time that she'd known the army captain, she'd never heard her say so much at once.

"Maybe that's our way in," she said.

"Takeout *pierogi*?" asked Beta, her eyes narrowing. "They will not open the door for a fake food delivery."

Olivia shook her head. "No, I'm thinking about soccer. There's a stadium nearby, right?" At Beta's nod, she continued. "Is there a game scheduled?"

Beta shrugged. "There is always a game scheduled. But *hlavy kysaného zelí* or no, they will not sneak out. They are stupid but not that stupid. And even if they did, Bryk would send more men to replace them."

Olivia sighed. "Once my team used mercaptan to fake a gas leak to get the target out of his house. That would be really useful right now. A team would be useful, too. What would you have done without me?"

Beta shrugged again. "I would have knocked on the door and announced that Bryk had sent me. Then I would have shot whoever answered and used his body as a shield while I shot the others."

Olivia laughed. "That would work, as long as his deadweight doesn't trap you. Or there's a guy in the toilet who comes out in time to shoot you. At best, you burn your cover with Bryk."

"I could wear a mask," said Beta.

Olivia laughed again. "Pretty sure Bryk has memorized your physique. Me, on the other hand ..." She paused, thinking. "How about the windows? They don't have bars. Do they have sensors?"

Beta shook her head.

"Cameras?"

"No." Beta leaned forward. "I told you, Bryk could leave the door open. Those guards are there on the theoretical possibility that someone tries to steal the women. And to kill them if the police are on the way."

Olivia sighed. "Look, the issue comes down to timing. The longer we can keep Bryk from sending reinforcements, the more likely we can get all of the women out of there. Do you think you can bluff your way in for a wellness check? You did say he put you in charge of watching over them."

Beta narrowed her eyes. "Perhaps. But how does that not burn me with Bryk?"

Now Olivia grinned. "If we do this right, Bryk will blame the *hlavy kysaného zelí*. And thank you in the process."

They split up at this point in the planning, Beta to do a little reconnaissance on the apartment and Olivia to investigate local sources for supplies and work through various scenarios given what they knew. Everything depended on good intel about the women.

The news wasn't encouraging.

"One of the women was pregnant and miscarried. She is bleeding steadily and complaining of nausea and fatigue," said Beta when she met with Olivia at Silesia Park a few hours later.

"She's not walking out," said Olivia.

Beta's gaze incinerated the air between them. "If we do not get her out soon, she will never walk out."

"Can you convince the men you've hijacked an ambulance to take her to the hospital?" asked Olivia, biting her lip as she thought. "I've had emergency medical training as well as in battlefield medicine."

By way of answer, Beta's upper lip lifted from her teeth.

"Okay, I'm sorry I asked," said Olivia.

She turned and started walking as she continued. Beta followed.

"This is our way in. I'll take care of sourcing an ambulance. I can play the role of paramedic, the one left behind when you assaulted the driver. Order one of the guards to help me carry her out. I'll prepare a syringe of something special for our gallant assistant to take him out of play."

Beta studied her a moment, clearly considering this tactic. "That takes care of one woman and one guard. What about the others?"

"Getting her out of there buys us some time for the next play."

"Which is?"

"Convincing the remaining guards to move the women. That's the only way for us to rescue all of them before Bryk can act. Make up whatever story you need to sell it. Say that the site is compromised. You need to sow a little suspicion between them while you do it. It will make it easier to manipulate them against each another. And to build an alibi for you."

A slow grin widened the Czech's mouth, though it only made her look feral. "That will not be difficult. They are like rabid dogs, snapping at each other's heels more often than not. But that does not mean they will move the women. They fear and idolize Bryk too much."

"Then leverage that. You need to convince them it's something that Bryk would want because of the market value of the women, which they've already compromised by so carelessly letting one woman die on the way to the hospital."

Beta stopped. "You have thought of everything." She clearly understood Olivia's ploy.

Olivia halted as well. "This way she'll be safe. And it gives you more influence in swaying the guards into moving the women quickly without checking in with Bryk first."

"It is a good thing that Bryk is too cheap to use proper surveillance. I will narrate my own dialogue for his video later."

Nodding, Olivia started walking again. "We'll hit them enroute to the new location. If we play it right, each man will swear to Bryk that the other sold him out to the competition. You'll return in time to throw doubt on both of them. They'll be so busy accusing each other that I'll be gone with the women before they can track us."

Beta sniffed. "It is not as satisfying as my approach, but it will do." It was as close to praise as the Czech captain was likely to give her.

"Understood." Humor colored Olivia's voice.

"Oh, and Beta?" When the other woman looked at her, she continued. "You'll need to help me sell my role as terrorized paramedic. How hard can you punch?"

NINE

Forty-five minutes later, Beta banged on the apartment door while holding a handgun at Olivia's back. Olivia wore the figure-obscuring orange-and-black Polish paramedic uniform and sported a fresh bruised cheek and split lip. She'd slicked her hair into a severe ponytail and slipped gray contacts from her go bag over her blue eyes. A stretcher sat along the wall in the hallway.

Beta stared up toward the WiFi camera mounted over the door until a pale, meaty-looking man shorter than she was opened it. As soon as he did, she shouldered the door wider, dragging Olivia with her. Olivia kept her face downcast, stumbling along so that her weight added to Beta's momentum. Bryk's man retreated back into the apartment.

Beta swiveled the gun towards him.

His eyes widened.

"We are here to collect the woman who is hemorrhaging," she said. Her cool voice belied her smoldering gaze.

She swept that incendiary look over the other two men in the living area of the small apartment. Olivia could have sworn she smelled smoke in its wake. The two sat stunned, one with a videogame controller and the other with a soda bottle raised partway to his mouth.

"This one"—here she pushed Olivia forward—"will make sure that she lives. If she does not, you all will tell Bryk why you are losing him money. And then you will face me."

After delivering this silky promise, she stepped forward and whipped her weapon across the short guard's face. He staggered backwards, his hand reaching for the cut that opened on his cheek.

Olivia scurried toward the closed bedroom door on the left where Beta had found the hemorrhaging woman on her wellness check.

"Get up, *dupek*," said Beta behind her. The slur sounded particularly vitriolic. A scrabbling sound followed. "You will help the paramedic put the woman on the stretcher in the hallway. Go!"

As Olivia opened the bedroom door, she heard him lurch into the hall outside. How Beta invested enough force to shove the heavier guard, Olivia could only guess. Either via sheer willpower or the natural terror inspired in her targets at her unholy glower.

At the thought, Olivia's fingers strayed to her St. Michael medal. It remained cool.

Beta called out to the guard. "Do not even think of running for help. I can shoot both of your friends and find you before you reach the next floor."

Okay, so perhaps he wasn't as intimidated as he seemed.

But there was little she could do now but trust her new partner to handle the three men.

Olivia shifted her focus to the woman lying on one of the two twin beds. Two women sat numb-faced on the other twin bed while a relatively sturdy-looking woman massaged the prone woman's abdomen. Although Olivia only had academic knowledge about hemorrhaging after a miscarriage, she recognized that what the woman was doing helped the most likely cause, uterine atony, that is, when the uterus muscles failed to contract fully.

She strode to the bed and set her emergency case down. "Keep massaging her abdomen," she said to the woman in Polish, "while I check her vital signs and start an IV."

Behind her, the stretcher's wheels rattled as the browbeaten guard maneuvered the mobile cot into the bedroom. She heard Beta berating the other men in the main room, listening as best she could while she opened her case for any signs of trouble. This little unsanctioned op could go pear-shaped at any moment.

If it did, she and Beta had no support in a city controlled by Bryk.

She worked quickly to stabilize the woman, who'd lapsed into unconsciousness. Olivia didn't know the woman's history, and even if she did, the ambulance that they'd hijacked hadn't been stocked with the typical drugs, such as oxytocin, used in conjunction with uterine massage to stop excessive bleeding. The best she could do was start transfusing O negative blood along with other fluids to keep the woman from going into hypovolemic shock.

When that was done, Olivia looked up at the guard, whose bleeding cheek and surly expression boded nothing good. Standing, she pulled some gauze from the case.

"Let me take care of you first," she said in a low voice, gesturing towards the laceration.

He looked startled and then suspicious. "Why?"

Olivia shrugged. "I need help getting her onto the gurney and lifting it into the ambulance. It will go faster if I give you something for the pain so you can focus."

"What is taking so long?" called Beta. She strode into view from the doorway. "You"—she glared at Olivia—"stop flirting and get her to the ambulance."

Olivia dropped her gaze, praying that the guard would take her up on the offer once they reached the ambulance.

They lifted the woman together onto the gurney while the other women watched. As Olivia packed up the case, she thanked the woman who'd been massaging the unconscious woman's uterus.

The other woman nodded, a dim glimmer of defiance in her gaze. "I learned it on my farm," she said in accented Polish. Olivia wondered which Eastern European country she was from. "We treated our cows better than these men do." She spat onto the floor.

Olivia wanted to assure her that she and Beta would free them from this slavery, but she could say nothing about their plans in front of the guard.

Slipping the pack's strap over her shoulder, she nodded at her reluctant helper, and they wheeled the patient to the elevator and then to the waiting ambulance. Olivia waited until they'd lifted the specially designed stretcher into the van and secured it to the inside before looking over her shoulder at the guard, whose twisted expression confirmed that his head hurt.

"Want to come up here and let me clean that for you?" she asked, nodding toward his cheek.

He squinted. "Can I get something for my head first?"

"Yes, just hop up and sit down here." Olivia patted the bench seat along the side of the van.

After he lumbered into the compartment and sat down, she pulled out the syringe that she'd filled with propofol, an anesthetic normally used via IV for surgery. It wasn't ideal for sedating someone you wanted to kidnap since it rarely did more than relax the individual when injected into a muscle, but she'd calculated a high enough dosage to knock him out long enough to start an IV drip with the same drug.

The *dupek* wasn't going anywhere but the hospital where he'd have a handwritten note pinned to his shirt assigning him responsibility for the woman's critical condition.

Olivia drove the ambulance to the closest ER, where she abandoned it in the entrance portico with its lights rolling.

Now to wait for phase two of this off-the-books mission.

Provided that Beta Czerná convinced Bryk's other two guards to move the rest of the women—and soon.

As it turned out, Beta's dark arts of persuasion worked just fine.

Not only that, but she'd cleverly persuaded the senior-most guard to arrange the transport at Bryk's expense.

Two hours after Olivia had dropped the first woman and her former captor off at the hospital, Beta called her from the truck-rental facility where Bryk's organization had an account for repeat business. Olivia found it hilarious in an "it hurts when I laugh" way that syndicates ran their businesses much as multinational corporations did. They even laundered, that is, 'managed' their money the same way with subsidiaries and shell corporations.

It would take a gifted and zealous team of accountants to trace all of Bryk's money despite no foreign bank accounts in his portfolio. Even then, the money often resided with extended family as cash and prepaid credit cards in a rough analog to a *hawaladar* network.

What she wouldn't give to disentangle this pernicious organism from the fabric of society.

Stop thinking about that, Olivia scolded herself. *Focus on getting the women out.*

What she would do with them after that, she didn't know, but being an operative meant being comfortable with ambiguous, rapidly evolving situations.

Drive west to Prague made the most sense ....

"The package will be on the road to Bytom within fifteen minutes."

"I'll be ready," said Olivia.

She checked her watch. The truck would reach the ambush point in roughly half an hour. It was early evening. Though the sun wouldn't set for another three hours, the overcast sky portended one of the regional thunderstorms that occurred this time of year. She wished that there were trees or powerlines along this stretch of road, anything she could bring down with a small charge that would block traffic.

Stopping a moving delivery truck filled with nearly catatonic sex victims in the storage compartment, on a main road, in heavy rain ... well, that was going to take some finesse.

And a whole lot of luck.

Olivia wrapped her hand around her St. Michael medal. *Think of me,* whispered *Sensei* Mark's voice in her memory.

"I wish you were here next to me," she said aloud.

The clouds parted along the horizon. A ray from the low-lying sun struck her rearview mirror and blinded her for a moment.

When the clouds shifted, deepening the light into early dusk, Olivia felt as if her mentor's shadowy presence filled the passenger seat in the stolen sedan. Her anxiety eased. She became hyper focused, staying calm even when the rain started. Fortunately, the traffic evaporated when it did.

Twenty minutes later, her phone rang. It was Beta.

"I am driving the white Škoda sedan. The truck is directly behind me."

"Copy that."

Olivia pulled the neck gaiter she wore over her nose and mouth and waited until the truck passed her. Then she pulled out behind it, leaving her headlights off. Up ahead, Beta accelerated into the passing lane, giving Olivia space to maneuver.

Olivia also accelerated, straddling the shoulder of the road as she brought her car up to match the speed of the truck until her front bumper aligned with its rear panel.

Thunder cracked overhead.

Then she swerved into the truck, tapping it. It pivoted around an imaginary axis and slowed to a stop off the road as she sped up. She veered into the right lane and pulled a U-turn on the empty road before coming back around to the stationary truck just as the skies opened up and rain fell in heavy sheets.

Slamming the brakes twenty meters away from the motionless vehicle, Olivia flung her door wide and sprinted to the cab where the driver had started to open his door. She planted her feet and aimed a combat shotgun at him.

"Tell your friend to stay put," she said, dropping her voice an octave and letting it go husky. "Or I shoot you full of lots of nasty bullet holes."

By the time Beta parked behind the truck, Bryk's two men had descended from the cab and donned zip-ties around their wrists before Olivia forced them to march toward tree cover at the side of the road. There a masked Beta injected each of them with flunitrazepam, otherwise known as the date-rape drug Rohypnol, that she'd sourced from Bryk's own supply at The Wild Stallion.

Then while she removed the GPS unit from the rental truck, Olivia led one of the men back to the cab. Beta dragged the other man with her to the Škoda, which she would drive north to Warsaw where Bryk's main rival operated.

They accomplished all of this in silence, only nodding when Beta marched the second man away. Though it was unlikely the guards could identify either of them in their drugged state along a dark, rainy road, neither Olivia nor Beta wanted the added risk.

Beta lifted a chin toward Olivia as she maneuvered the stumbling guard past the truck. Five minutes later the deluge swallowed them.

Olivia turned to the man slumped against the passenger door.

"Stay," she growled.

He flinched so hard he hit his head on the window and passed out.

That had to hurt.

She jumped down and went to the back of the truck where she lifted the door before pulling the neck gaiter down. Rain washed over her bare cheeks.

Eight faces like moons stared back at her.

"You're safe now," she said. "I'm taking you far from Kacper Bryk and his people."

A woman shifted from the back of the group. Her face in the gray twilight looked familiar.

It was the woman who'd massaged the miscarrying woman's abdomen. Recognition lit her wary gaze, but a tentative smile fled before it could transform her face.

Olivia didn't wait for the question she saw forming on the other woman's lips.

"She's alive. When I'm done with him, Bryk will wish he'd never hurt any of you."

Lightning cracked overhead in a brilliant display.

In that moment, Olivia knew it was true. Just as she knew that Beta Czerná would be at her side to take the Polish crime lord down.

Olivia returned three days later to the Prague field office. Almost as soon as she entered the building, her senses started buzzing. Something was up.

She was in the middle of writing her after-action report when the station manager came to her office door. At Reardon's side stood one of the security officers that the Agency employed to monitor the physical building.

"Markham, come with me."

Olivia looked up from her keyboard. "Sure," she said, forcing a casualness she didn't feel into her voice.

Reardon led her to the same airless conference room where she'd sat shivering after the adrenaline from their escape from Mszana had burned away. At least then Reardon had been compassionate enough to allow her hot coffee and a thermal blanket around her shoulders.

Not so much today.

He gestured Olivia toward a chair but didn't take one himself. Instead, he paced around the small room. The security officer hadn't entered, but Olivia knew that he stood at the ready in the hall. On the lacquered table in front of her sat an ominous dark dossier. Hers?

At last, when anxiety had started to fill Olivia's stomach with cold acid, Reardon turned and looked at her.

"How long have you been with the Agency?"

Olivia knew this was rhetorical. Reardon had definitely turned her employment file into bedtime reading while she was gone.

"I joined fulltime in the spring of 2010," she said, carefully choosing her details.

"You know Sam Ahren?" he asked without preamble. He looked a little incredulous.

"Yes, he recruited me to the CIA. I trained under him."

Olivia left off that that her recruitment hadn't been standard operating procedure and that one result was that she and Sam outed a CIA case officer in the Special Activities Division who ran ghost assets. She'd then worked under Sam on special internal investigations related to SAD and their Special Forces recruits. It was the primary reason she'd been able to have her pick of fieldwork placement, leading her to the high-profile team with Thomas.

Reardon said nothing for a moment.

"That explains a lot," he said at last, sitting across from her.

He didn't clarify his cryptic remark, but Olivia knew enough to realize that it rankled the Prague station chief that there were large swathes of her personnel file to which he didn't have access.

She waited, but when Reardon still didn't say anything, she said, "Did you have something to share with me?" She tipped her chin to indicate the thick folder.

"What I have to share with you is this: I'm not Sam Ahren. I don't have time for divas or field officers who think that their judgment trumps mine. First, you worm your way into a mission you had no business being involved in—and over my objections—and then you nearly get the team leader killed. What possessed you to let a civilian intercede in your operation?"

"Who?" asked Olivia.

"The man who carried Sergeant Major Jonas from the SUV."

An icy thrill went through her.

She had been clear during the briefing that she would never have been able to extricate the sergeant major from the SUV—or turn it into an IED.

"If you're asking why I trusted him, that's a hard one to answer. My gut is the short answer. The long answer is that he reminded me of my college karate instructor who had a lot to do with me going into the CIA. Either way, I didn't really have a choice, did I?"

"So you say."

"What does Sergeant Major Jonas say?" asked Olivia, her heartrate picking up several notches at Reardon's cold tone.

"He told his teammates that the Archangel Michael rescued him."

Olivia's fingertips went to her St. Michael medal before she could stop them. "Sergeant Major Jonas lost a lot of blood. And we were getting ready to drop a pineapple grenade into a tank of gas. Maybe it was a little wishful thinking on his part."

She hadn't wanted to question their good fortune before this, but Nate's rescue had been nothing short of a miracle....

Reardon shook his head. "Whatever it was, we haven't been able to find this good Samaritan and make sure he keeps what happened to himself. Not exactly ideal operational security, Markham."

He paused. Olivia didn't know what to say, so she kept her mouth shut and watched him. He held her gaze for several uncomfortable moments before setting his fingertips on the dossier.

"Nor is it ideal operational security for a lone field officer to return to the site of her most recent operation on some misguided quest."

Olivia sat up straight. "What quest is that?" she asked.

Her mouth was dry, but she refused to lick her lips or swallow. Reardon's hawkish gaze watched her for the slightest slip, but she wasn't about to give him anything if she could help it.

Reardon opened the folder to reveal a photo of Beta in the café in Chorzów.

"Whatever it is, it has something to do with this woman."

Ice threatened to choke Olivia. "Did you have me followed?" she asked.

Her gut told her that Reardon didn't know Beta's identity. He clearly hadn't been read in on the D-Boys' Czech military contact.

Now Reardon's surveillance threatened not only Olivia's future at the CIA. It threatened Beta's future with Czech army intelligence. If Bryk didn't kill her first.

Olivia couldn't let that happen.

"She's a friend," she said nonchalantly without looking at the dossier again. "We had coffee as your surveillance shows."

"Would this friend have anything to do with the truckload of women who suddenly appeared yesterday at a small U.S. Army base in Ansbach, Germany?"

A pulse beat a staccato at the base of Olivia's throat. "You seem to have all the answers, Reardon. Why bother questioning me?"

Olivia almost missed the glimmer in her boss's gaze. But she didn't. All at once she knew what he was trying to do.

"Oh, you don't. Have all the answers. Am I right?" She leaned forward and reached for the dossier.

Reardon snatched the folder from her reach. Olivia didn't need to see its contents to know what it held: nothing but the photo of Beta on top of a stack of scrap paper. It was a classic interrogation ploy. He'd made his play and lost.

Olivia had almost confessed to save Beta. She would have betrayed her instead.

She sat back, crossed her arms over her chest, and watched Reardon through narrowed eyes.

"That's how you're going to play this then?" her boss asked. His gaze flicked to the corner.

He's videorecording this little interview, thought Olivia. She said nothing.

"You leave me no choice, Markham. You're removed from duty pending a review of your recent actions in Poland, including your unsanctioned foray there in the past three days. If we find what I think we'll find, you're through at the Agency."

He leaned forward, malice glittering in his gaze now. "Don't bother contacting your only friend in the CIA. Sam Ahren disappeared while undercover in Albania, and no one knows where he is."

TEN

Olivia turned in her security badge and said goodbye to the few acquaintances she'd made in the Prague field office in the short time she'd been stationed there. Although she was technically on indefinite leave from fieldwork, Reardon hadn't directed her to return Stateside while he conducted his witch hunt into her actions.

She was in limbo.

She suspected that her boss hoped that she'd just fade away without a fight. Or, better, planned to tail her throughout Prague in order to pad his case against her. Even without Sam Ahren's powerful backing, Reardon needed more than innuendo to get rid of her.

He really had been out of the field too long if he thought either of those tactics would work. Or maybe it was as her father had always said: *managers could neither do nor teach.*

Despite Reardon's warning not to bother contacting Sam, Olivia tried anyway. Sam had given her a VOIP number that he forwarded to whatever Company or mission phone he carried. He'd also set up a dummy email account on all of the major ISPs with shared login and password for Olivia, much like the shared account she'd set up for Marina Orlova on the dating site.

But Sam, who'd always responded within two hours of a message in any of these venues, remained silent. As far as Olivia could tell, he hadn't even accessed the email accounts.

Worry sat heavily on her shoulders, more for her Company mentor than for herself.

For herself, well, she knew exactly how to play Reardon.

Olivia logged into the dating site and composed a message for her erstwhile asset.

And then she took herself to the movies.

Mission: Impossible—Ghost Protocol, the blockbuster starring American movie star Tom Cruise whose opening scene had been filmed near Prague, still played in local theaters.

She couldn't remember the last time she'd seen a movie, let alone bought a ticket, popcorn, and soda and plopped into a seat in the middle of a nearly empty theater during a matinee.

Probably in high school, before her cousin Emily's boyfriend strangled her.

Olivia propped her feet on the back of the seat in front of her and got lost in the high-octane action of super spies out in the cold after being blamed for bombing the Kremlin by a master villain. When the U.S. president invokes Ghost Protocol—publicly disavowing the Impossible Missions Force—Ethan Hunt and his team race to save the world without resources or backup. Of course, doing so would clear their names and bring them back into the official IMF fold.

Olivia had just watched Ethan scaling Dubai's Burj Khalifa, the world's tallest building, wearing a pair of prototype high-tech gloves when Marina sat in the seat next to hers.

Olivia allowed herself a small sigh.

Spies as superheroes. What she wouldn't give for some magical tech like those electro-adhesive gloves ....

At last, she popped a few kernels of popcorn into her mouth, chewed, and then said to Marina, "Popov got paid."

"I know," said the Russian asset, lighting a cigarette. "He has been back to Prague already to celebrate."

"His buyer did not take possession of the package, however."

Marina looked out of the corner of her eye at Olivia before facing forward and blowing smoke. "That is good" is all she said.

Olivia sipped her soda before continuing, her gaze on the screen as IMF agent Jane Carter kicked the French *femme fatale* out a window of the skyscraper. "Which means that you have been very useful to American interests. We'd like to continue our relationship."

"Go on," said Marina without looking at Olivia.

She already had excellent instincts this one. Reardon didn't deserve to inherit her.

Olivia turned her face toward the other young woman. "Have you realized yet how much we look alike?"

Marina shifted in her seat. Her gaze slid sideways, lending her features a sly aspect in the flickering projector light. "You will have to smoke, I am afraid, darling."

Olivia sighed and popped a buttered kernel into her mouth. Yes, she'd have to smoke.

As Olivia had suspected, Marina proved adept at the cloak-and-dagger skulduggery in which her American handler asked her to engage. She gamely switched clothes with Olivia in the theater's bathroom, pulling her long blond hair into an American-style ponytail and tugging Olivia's Boston Red Sox cap low on her brow. She passed her cigarettes to Olivia with an audible sigh, but Olivia thought Marina rather enjoyed the challenge of denying her addiction.

As Olivia had also surmised, someone tailed her. She watched as Marina walked through the lobby, her arm swinging and her stride loose in a fair approximation of Olivia's. A short man wearing a gray polo shirt, black pants and shoes, and a light-colored windbreaker moved out of the shifting group of people near the concession stand. He threw his popcorn into the trash and followed Marina through the large glass doors. When she left the cinema and turned east toward the river, he did likewise.

Bartos. Olivia recognized him as a local pavement artist that Reardon had on call, someone who didn't mind informing to the Americans.

Olivia refrained from snorting to herself. The station chief clearly didn't realize that his junior field officer had read through all of the station's most recent case files, including Bogdi Król's, to gain context for the graymail that she vetted. That's how she knew that Reardon had used the Czech informant extensively for local intelligence gathering. Among uninteresting dirt on Czech criminals, Bartos had spotted the Polish facilitator in Prague in the weeks leading up to the nuclear deal with Popov.

Olivia shadowed the Czech, running her own SDR the whole time. As she'd figured, Reardon hadn't put a team on her. He'd likely funded Bartos's surveillance via a discretionary account.

Keeping a discreet distance—no more than twenty meters—Olivia followed Reardon's minion as he trailed her stand-in. Marina performed admirably for someone with no formal training, rerunning the SDR that Olivia had run during their first meeting. The young Russian asset dawdled in front of clothing stores before pausing in front of a nail salon and then entering as Olivia had instructed. As expected, Bartos took up a post across the street where he could watch the entrance to the salon.

Having detected no other watchers, Olivia made her way to the 26 tram, which she took north over the Vltava River to the Holešovice neighborhood where Beta had a one-bedroom apartment. The military intelligence officer had given Olivia a key so that they could meet without prying eyes and ears.

Olivia arrived before Beta. She had no intention of snooping, but being alone in the space would give her time to absorb more details on her new clandestine partner. As she sat on the hard gray sofa, she looked around the small living space. No pictures, no extra, soft throw pillows. No TV. It was very clean and spare. Functional, but spare. Like those long-term residential suites available in the U.S. for relocated employees while they house hunted.

Nothing here supported a legend or even that someone called this place home.

Because it wasn't.

And yet Olivia knew it was the actual personal residence of the taciturn Czech officer, who'd both trusted Olivia enough to give her access and at the same time had revealed no vulnerabilities. No connections, no memories, no love.

A bittersweet pang of compassion and recognition caught Olivia off guard.

Would she end up like Beta?

Toying with her St. Michael medal, Olivia's thoughts drifted toward her family back in the States. It had been more than a year since she'd seen them. Perhaps she should go home ...

The sound of the key in the lock of the apartment door brought her attention back to her surroundings.

A moment later, Beta's glossy dark curls appeared as she nudged the door open with a motorcycle helmet. The tall Czech wore black leather from head to toe. Despite her slender build, the clothing along with the chunky black motorcycle boots lent a dangerous edge to her presence. Heavy leather protected against wipeouts on pavement and knife attacks.

Olivia remembered the karambit, now safely tucked inside her own ankle boot. She also remembered the deep laceration she'd suffered when a terrorist had stabbed her during an attack on an Ibiza beach four years ago, nearly to the day. She placed a palm against her abdomen where an astonishingly faint scar was all that remained of the vicious assault. Swimsuits aren't much protection against tactical knives. Thank God Sam and his team had arrived when they did.

Another miracle whispered in her thoughts.

Beta dropped the helmet on the breakfast bar facing the galley kitchen as she toed the door closed behind her. Despite her gear and her profession, her move had all the grace of a ballerina.

"What are you wearing?" she asked as she looked at Olivia.

Olivia shrugged. "What all chic young administrative assistants wear at the Russian embassy."

Beta telegraphed a question with a raised eyebrow.

"Our little escapade in Chorzów didn't go unnoticed. I had to sneak out of my dad's house because I've been grounded. My body double today is a Russian asset I cultivated."

"You would like to drink Trebitsch with me then?" said Beta, turning away to open a cabinet.

Inside Olivia glimpsed a half-empty bottle of the Czech single-malt whisky and a single highball glass. Before she could answer, Beta pulled out both and poured a generous serving before walking over and holding it out to her. Olivia accepted the glass. Beta tipped the bottle to her lips and drank.

Olivia sipped the whisky. It had a malty sweetness as of fresh fruit. She was no connoisseur, but she detected an alcoholic sharpness that kept the whisky from being mild and smooth. It seemed an ideal drink for Beta.

Beta held the Trebitsch by the bottleneck. "She will have to be your understudy."

Olivia nodded. "She says Popov is back. He seems to like the money that Król brings him."

"Król often sends Bryk business." Beta pulled out one of the stools at the breakfast bar and sat, the Trebitsch bottle at her elbow on the counter next to her. "They attended the same Catholic primary school."

"Where they learned all the best techniques to become master criminals," said Olivia drily before draining her whisky. She set the empty glass on the bare coffee table in front of her.

Beta shrugged. "Some are simply bad seeds, no matter what education and example they are given."

Olivia found Beta's cynicism a little shocking, but then she remembered Jin, who'd strangled Emily. He'd been a teenager from a good family in a wealthy suburb of Boston.

"Yep, some are just bad seeds," she said. Sighing, she shoved the memory aside. Time to get down to business. "It seems I'm at loose ends for an indefinite period of time, so I can focus on our operation. As long as Reardon doesn't get wind of what I'm doing. Then I'll be a free agent."

"Will your asset be able to provide an alibi? I suggest a trip. Many Czechs visit Croatia, although Greece is farther yet."

"Hm," said Olivia, considering the suggestion. "I've always wanted to visit Greece. That could work, but I'd need a document forger. Marina can pass as me with the local man Reardon hired, but that won't suffice for traveling."

"That is simple," said Beta, waving her hand dismissively. "Making Bryk bleed for sex trafficking is not. Do you have any ideas?"

Pursing her lips, Olivia tilted her head. "Whatever we do, I'd love to take Popov off the board. He's willing to sell stolen nukes to terrorists." Then she sighed. "But it's just the two of us, even if your handler is on board with disrupting Bryk's network. It'll take a minor miracle to do more."

Beta shrugged. "You think too expansively. I am perfectly happy to hijack the next delivery truck of women scheduled this week."

Olivia leaned forward. "Tell me."

And for the next hour she and Beta discussed tactics.

As intended, Bryk now thought that one of his competitors had made a bold move to steal from him. He promoted Beta, who'd narrated the events on the surveillance video, to run his trafficking operation. The guards, he executed.

Beta was now in the perfect position. Not only would she have detailed information about the victims and the infrastructure around their trafficking, but she had Bryk's ear. Paranoia, especially of his own employees and associates, fueled a criminal of his stature.

Bryk wouldn't suspect Beta. She had no connections, criminal or otherwise, that he could discern. And the only thing that appeared to motivate her were the women he sold into sexual slavery.

It would be relatively simple to manipulate Bryk to target other criminals for the rescues that she and Olivia pulled off, all the while getting closer to him, feeding his paranoia. Pushing him to overreact to ghost threats.

It was how major powers had toppled dictators for decades. Hell, it had been going on throughout recorded history. Even King Théoden had his Wormtongue in Tolkien's epic fantasy.

At this thought, Olivia glanced at Beta, who finished the whisky in a long pull on the bottle.

No, she shook her head. *Beta is no flattering sycophant. She is more an Iago. She'd stab Bryk in the eye, and he'd still call her honest.*

Of course, Olivia was their secret weapon.

Prague was less than a five-hour drive to Katowice. After their meeting on tactics, Olivia gave Beta's document forger a two-for-one deal: a U.S. passport in her name with Marina's picture and a Czech passport for her with the alias *Emílie Novak*. While Marina enjoyed the beaches and seafood in Santorini, Mykonos, and Corfu, Olivia set up temporary base at Beta's apartment. She'd have to get a spray tan later. ...

Three days after being suspended, Olivia returned to Katowice to undertake reconnaissance of the tenement building that Bryk had designated as his new holding pen. The nondescript building, on 3

Maja Street not far from Szewczyk Square and the new train station, had the latest in video surveillance and reinforced-steel entry doors.

And only Beta knew the location.

"Do you need to supervise the delivery?" asked Olivia.

"What are you thinking?" asked Beta.

They'd met at the city's Market Square, which was really a confluence of three different markets. Given the fine May afternoon, the cafés with their awning-covered tables bustled with tourists and employees on their lunch break.

"I'm thinking that you'd make a fine overwatch."

Beta nodded and shifted as their server set a dish of *gołąbki*, a dish of stuffed cabbage rolls with a side of boiled potatoes and slathered in tomato sauce, in front of her. Despite her slender build, she had a hearty appetite and dug in.

Olivia herself found that the risk of operating against official sanction had whetted her own hunger. She had no problem finishing her generous helping of *bigos*, a stew of chopped meat, sauerkraut, and fresh, shredded cabbage while washing it down with a bottle of Żubr, the most popular Polish beer.

Somehow their tactical meeting had morphed into a lunch with a friend. A prickly, laconic friend, but a friend nevertheless.

A memory of Monica laughing at a stupid joke that Bryce had told during one of the interminable days they'd staffed the surveillance post hooked Olivia under the breastbone. She missed the former Army communications officer, even though she'd tried to suffocate the pain. Worse, she longed for the camaraderie that she'd experienced during her very first mission with Monica and the CIA. She'd been chasing that feeling ever since.

She and Beta settled on a plan to stage a fake detour on the route the delivery truck would follow to the tenement. This would be ludicrously easy given the ongoing construction of the new railway station, which had already missed its first completion deadline. It also meant leveraging their talents and limited resources to the fullest. To minimize the risk to innocent bystanders, Beta scheduled the transport for early morning.

After that, the operation became almost routine.

Olivia, masked and armed with two tactical FN P90 submachine guns with 50-round magazines, waited at the chokepoint where the traffic cones and signs diverted the short caravan of three vehicles. As soon as the lead vehicle stopped on the manhole cover under which she'd planted a small charge, she detonated it. Before the car stopped rocking from the explosion, Olivia followed it with an extended spray of bullets, pinning the occupants inside.

Meanwhile, Beta, who'd taken up overwatch on an unfinished upper floor in the nearby train station, shot out the tires on the rear vehicle. When the driver opened his door, she shot the sideview mirror. He closed it again.

Bryk's flunkeys got the idea. They needed to stay inside their vehicles.

Olivia confiscated the traffickers' cellphones and jammed the door locks with key blanks. After that, she disabled the two escort vehicles by sending dozens of rounds into their engines.

The cars and their occupants had been immobilized.

Then Olivia compelled the truck driver into the trunk of the follow car before driving the truck away.

This time, she met a representative of an NGO called New Hope that helped trafficked victims in Poland, many of them from Eastern

Europe. The woman, a Brit, helped Olivia and Beta transfer the fifteen scared teenagers to her van. She would drive them to a New Hope safe house in Germany before first light.

While Olivia transferred the young women to New Hope's care, Beta returned to The Wild Stallion. She was there when one of the escorts staggered into the bar with the tale of the hijacking. Bryk, furious, ordered his men to search for the truck and the hijackers.

They didn't have to go far.

As Bryk and his men hustled to grab guns and ammunition, the empty truck crashed into several parked cars before plowing into the bar's front window. A message spray painted in red on the truck's side read *I'M COMING FOR YOU*.

Olivia wished that she could have seen Bryk's reaction. Instead, she returned early the next morning to Prague, slipping into her apartment for the first time in more than a week.

The one-bedroom rental exuded a cool, musty smell that enveloped Olivia as she flipped on the overhead light. Something sent her nerves buzzing even before she saw the thick manila packet on the round breakfast table next to the galley kitchen.

Dropping her large duffel onto the floor inside the doorway, she pulled out her handgun, holding it in a two-handed grip as she scanned the living area for other signs of an intruder or boobytrap. Nothing stood out.

She looked in the tiny white-tiled bathroom and the bedroom, including the closet and under the bed, before returning to the manila envelope.

On the front, *Olivia* had been written in large, elegant letters. Inside she found an extensive file on a Serbian arms dealer named

Goran Savik, whom Italian foreign intelligence currently surveilled in Venice.

Her unknown source had also included classified American intelligence—also from an unknown source—showing that Savik had a Predator drone.

But the *pièce de résistance?*

Photos of Savik meeting with various criminals and terrorists, including Mr. X.

Sighing, Olivia set her 9mm down on the table and went into the kitchen to pour herself a gin-and-tonic. Then she sat down and began to study the intelligence packet.

On administrative leave or not, it looked like she was going to Venice.

ELEVEN

Olivia arrived in Venice that evening.

Before leaving Prague, she'd contacted Anastasia Fiore, the operative named in her mysterious packet as a member of the Italian surveillance team watching Savik. There had been enough details, including photos and NOC information, that Olivia believed that Signorina Fiore really was an officer of the *Agenzia Informazioni e Sicurezza Esterna* or AISE.

But she'd still called Sam, who again didn't answer or return her voicemail. And there was no one she could tap at the Prague field station that she trusted to keep her query from Reardon. Instead, she reached out to Beta, whose contacts confirmed the Italian spy's identity.

When Olivia called Signorina Fiore, she left out that she'd been placed on administrative leave, saying only that the Company had an interest in Savik. She didn't know what she'd do if the Italian investigated her and then refused to meet.

As it was, the Italian operative's initial response shocked Olivia.

"*Che meraviglia!* You can join me tonight at a masquerade at Savik's palazzo." Signorina Fiore paused for a fraction of a second before saying, "I do hope you have something to wear."

Olivia's wardrobe included an evening gown. She just hadn't thought she'd get access to Savik so quickly.

Tamping down her surprise, she said, "Of course. No mask, I'm afraid."

"Not to worry," said Signorina Fiore. "I can supply you with one. Shall we meet for drinks in the hotel bar at 9 p.m. to discuss our mutual interests?"

Olivia agreed and threw up a silent plea to the heavens that her approach would succeed. She had to follow up on these leads. Either someone was playing her—quite possibly Reardon, who had access to her previous mission in Berlin—or she had an unknown friend in the American intelligence community who didn't want Reardon involved.

Either way, Olivia needed to verify the packet's contents. And the only way to do that was to get access to Savik.

After packing her evening gown and grabbing her false Czech passport, Olivia drove to the Marriott hotel in Santa Croce, the district southwest of the Grand Canal that ran through Venice, and booked a room. After a room-service dinner, she went to the bar, where Signorina Fiore already waited at a table. As Olivia approached, the other woman stood to greet her.

The diminutive Italian looked nothing like an intelligence officer in Olivia's estimation, unless looking like a 1960s Bond-style spy counted. Her lustrous hair, the color of rich caramel, fell to her shoulders in soft waves. A distinctive divot in her chin counterbalanced her large, almond-shaped hazel eyes. And she was dressed in a black dress with flowing skirt that hugged her curves.

But Olivia's trained eye evaluated the other woman's easy grace and lean figure. By her estimation, Signorina Fiore could handle herself in hand-to-hand combat if the micro 9mm in her sequined clutch failed to stop her opponent—though Olivia doubted the other woman missed often, if indeed it ever came to that. If necessary, she'd use the knife strapped to her inner thigh.

Signorina Fiore gripped Olivia's hand with both of hers before leaning in and pressing featherlight kisses on Olivia's cheeks. A sophisticated perfume wafted velvety scents of vanilla-musk across Olivia, wrapping her in an invisible hug.

Olivia blinked a few times in astonishment. She'd never felt so comfortable so quickly with anyone before. It was almost as though she and the Italian operative had been good friends for years.

When she leaned back, Signorina Fiore smiled. It made her eyes sparkle. "Ms. Markham! It is *so* good to meet you. I must confess that you are not what I expected given your station chief's description."

And there it was. At least Signorina Fiore hadn't kept Olivia waiting. Or beat around the bush.

"And what would that be, Signorina Fiore?"

"That you are an entitled female of little ability willing to risk mission objectives to further her own interests."

Ouch. That stung.

Olivia blinked. "I guess that's one way to interpret my attitude and actions."

Signorina Fiore watched Olivia, the warm smile evaporating. "Yet some of your other colleagues speak very highly of you. It is difficult to know what to believe."

Olivia wondered who had vouched for her. She brushed her curiosity aside. "Does this mean that you are retracting the offer to take me to Savik's masquerade?"

"No." The other woman continued to regard her, as if she could read beneath Olivia's carefully composed veneer.

"Why?"

Signorina Fiore shrugged. "Because I trust my own judgment over all others. I find that one can learn a great deal about an operative in the field that cannot be gleaned from files and colleagues."

"Trial by fire then?" asked Olivia, a bitter note edging her question.

Signorina Fiore sighed. "For me as well, *bella*."

A loaded silence descended between them.

The Italian foreign intelligence officer broke it.

She leaned forward as if sharing a confidence. "But the real reason I invited you is for some—how do you Americans say?—moral support." She laughed. "Conflicting or not, no one has ever spoken about *my* fieldwork with such high praise."

Olivia doubted that had anything to do with Signorina Fiore's skill. If anything, the Italian operative wanted to be underestimated. And for some reason she wanted to boost Olivia's ego relative to her standing with the Italian team. Astonishingly, the almost-measurable pressure that surrounded them dissipated.

Whatever the reason, Olivia had passed the first hurdle.

"Olivia. Please call me Olivia," she said as she continued taking stock of the other woman, who'd lifted an almost imperceptible chin at a nearby waiter.

Signorina Fiore looked at her. "And you should call me Stasia."

"Of course."

Olivia gestured toward the low chairs and table that Stasia had claimed earlier. They sat.

"Where did you learn to speak English? You sound almost American. Your vowels are a little too round, though."

Stasia made a deprecating wave with her hands, but Olivia saw the slight shift in the other woman's posture. Olivia's observation surprised her.

"I spent some time in the U.S. when I was an adolescent," she said, dismissing the topic.

They chatted about the local wines and the best place to find gelato as if they were indeed old friends meeting for a casual drink before dinner. Once the waiter had dropped off a fresh *negroni* for Stasia and Olivia's rose-infused gin cocktail, however, the two women spoke about the Serbian arms dealer and the upcoming approach at his invitation-only masquerade.

Italian foreign intelligence had monitored Savik for months. The itinerant Serb liked to party wherever he negotiated major deals with buyers, but discovering the location of his secure rental properties had proven impossible for intelligence organizations.

Until now.

Stasia had patiently cultivated Savik's younger son, Vedran, a man who felt that his father and older brother didn't value his capabilities the way that they should. *He* was the weak link in Savik's operation. Stasia had worked Vedran's fragile ego until he believed that he'd shrewdly identified an urgent business opportunity to buy high-quality Semtex. He even thought it was his idea to bring her and a friend to his father's Venetian palazzo.

Not only did AISE have the address, they had a masterful operative on Savik's guest list.

"What about our weapons? Won't they be checking guests?"

Stasia's hazel eyes sparkled. "Vedran wouldn't allow the help to search his girlfriend." She tossed her head. "Besides, we do not need them, *bella*. Do we?"

Olivia grinned. She rather liked being the Trojan Horse this time.

She and Stasia walked the short distance to a side canal where a luxury motorboat crewed by Italian operatives in civilian clothing waited to ferry them to Savik's rental in Canareggio, the city's northernmost district. On the way, Stasia briefed Olivia about Venice's absentee homeowners, the world's elite who only cared about the address and not the fact that the city slowly sank into the lagoon, subletting their residences to anyone willing to pay.

When they arrived at the palazzo, two heavily muscled men in suits would have frisked them within an inch of their lives except that Vedran appeared and ordered the guards to stop.

Stasia aimed a wide smile at Olivia that said *I told you so*.

Despite being almost midnight, dozens of well-dressed, chattering partygoers greeted them inside the brightly lit palazzo.

"I will distract Savik," said Stasia in a low voice to Olivia as Vedran led her by the hand toward his father, "while you survey our host's lovely home."

Olivia nodded, though she wondered how well she would blend into the background in her bright azure evening gown.

As it happened, quite well when Stasia turned the full wattage of her charm on their thuggish host, pulling many of the guests into her orbit also.

Time for Olivia to go gray as CIA 101 had taught her.

She wended her way through the crowd, pulling a drink from a server's tray and nodding in a vague way, much as the Queen of England did when she waved at her adoring subjects. Within half an hour, she'd traversed all of the rooms on the first floor and catalogued all of the staff and security personnel, identifying the most vulnerable points for entry and those guards who could be removed without an immediate alert.

In the back of one of the main rooms on the ground floor, she found a locked four-meter-high carved door. AISE's plans showed that the room beyond had been used as an office by the owners. She'd need to return later to recover the data on Stasik's buyers. It was unlikely that Mr. X would be at the event this evening....

No one seemed to notice her snooping until she approached the stairs, which were tucked toward the back of the empty entrance hall. The guard stationed there blocked them with his massive bulk, his hands crossed at his waist and his glare implacable.

Olivia strode confidently toward him anyway. She'd found that tactic often worked, especially with muscular men who underestimated her.

This guard didn't.

He shifted in front of her as she lifted her foot to the lowest step, dropping a heavy hand on her forearm.

"No."

He said nothing else, likely because he only spoke Serbian. But his flinty gaze said everything. He wouldn't hesitate to hurt her if she persisted.

That told her two things.

First, Savik hid something from public consumption. Something valuable and likely deadly.

Second, they weren't getting up there without a fight.

"What's wrong, *bella*?" asked Goran Savik, reeking of tobacco and vodka, as he leaned toward Anastasia Fiore with a heavy hand on her lower back.

Savik's thick, wet lips brushed her ear as he spoke. His harsh whisper was anything but. Several people nearby looked at them in open curiosity.

Stasia quelled the tremor of revulsion that threatened to roll through her. She and the Serbian arms dealer stood with his sons Aco and Vedran in the 17th-Century palazzo's loggia room along with a few dozen prospective buyers and two of his men, who were conspicuously armed. The Serbs, dressed in black, made her think of monstrous crows among the room's green *marmorino* plaster, Baroque gold-framed oil paintings, and delicate furniture.

Smiling, Stasia forced herself to focus on Savik instead of the western entry to the loggia where Olivia Markham had appeared moments before. The other operative's face under her embellished half mask gave nothing away, but Stasia read tension in her shoulders.

She turned her full gaze on Savik, the wattage of her smile undimmed even as she breathed through her mouth. "I am afraid that my drink is empty." As she spoke, she raised her cocktail glass, which she'd emptied into a large vase of fresh flowers before stepping into his presence.

Savik lifted his chin at one of his men who stood nearby. The man's face showed no resentment at being sent to get Stasia another drink. Rumor had it that Savik paid loyalty exceptionally well—and punished disloyalty in equal measure.

What would he do if he discovered that he'd exposed his soft underbelly to the woman before him, the one who'd manipulated his slow-witted son for the opportunity?

At that thought, Stasia let the tips of her fingers trail along the edge of her thigh, where her combat dagger—an ARDA special edition used by the 17th Raiders Wing of the Italian Special Forces—hid just beneath the surface of her skirt.

Savik sipped his vodka from a cut-crystal tumbler, which he held with sausage-like fingers. His dark eyes glittered as he appraised her. "Tell me, Signorina, how is it that you have convinced my brainless son Vedran that he has *any* hope of satisfying someone of your—how shall I describe them?—obvious charms?"

Stasia laughed, the merry sound caressing the air around them. Savik almost visibly relaxed. Vedran, who stood next to her, stiffened, however. Exuding sympathy, Stasia laid a hand on his forearm, and he, too, relaxed. She needed him to stay focused on their plan to tell his father about her business proposition. After that, she wouldn't have to smooth his ruffled feathers anymore.

She looked at Savik under her eyelashes and said, "Signore, you would not want me to kiss and tell."

Olivia, who'd been making her way through the crowd with demure grace and murmured apologies, stepped into the space between the two sons, whose gazes never left Stasia.

Stasia was impressed. Despite being alluring in a peacock-blue gown that clung to her lithe figure, the American had moved through the palace rooms without attracting undue attention. It was a talent that was hard to train. And perhaps all the more intriguing given her standing at the American intelligence agency.

What other talents did this American operative have?

Stasia didn't know what prompted her to work with Olivia after she'd discovered that the American had misled her. But something about the CIA station chief's disavowal had irked her. Stasia hadn't gotten to where she was leading an AISE team without trusting her gut about people and situations. And Reardon set her antennae buzzing.

Still, she hadn't been entirely forthcoming with Olivia about tonight's operation. It wasn't a simple infiltration for intelligence gathering as she'd implied to the American field officer. It was a full-bore mission to snatch Savik and his sons.

It really would be trial by fire. And Stasia would get burned if her instincts failed her now.

She had a lot of maneuvering to do before signaling for special forces to drop onto the roof and come through the front door. But it would take time to rid the palazzo of Savik's guests and take control of the arms dealer's men.

Stasia needed to know what had set off Olivia's radar.

Let us see if she can follow my lead.

One of the servants approached with a drink tray, including Stasia's favored *negroni*. As she turned to reach for the glass, Stasia shifted closer to the servant and pulled the *negroni* towards her, deliberately unbalancing the tray of full drinks. They tumbled to the floor as the poor woman cried out, spraying Stasia with ice and alcohol.

Before Stasia could flutter her hands and exclaim that she needed to escape to the women's toilet to clean up, Vedran backhanded the servant. The young woman stumbled backwards and fell to one knee, flinging a hand onto a wingback chair to stop from going all the way down.

Stasia's temper flared. Time to change the dynamics. It was always best to go with the flow, anyway.

Slipping out of her stiletto heels before jumping into the chair, she pivoted to lunge onto Vedran's back, catching him—and everyone around him—off guard. She pressed the ARDA dagger into his side.

Silence descended over the party like a thunderclap.

Stasia, her arm wrapped around his son's neck, said to Savik, "You are right, *bello*. My charms are too good for one such as your son."

From her peripheral vision, she saw that Olivia had followed her lead and disarmed Savik's bodyguard, who now lay sprawled on the floor at her feet. She aimed the gun at Aco, whose glower promised violence.

Savik threw his head back and laughed. The heavy tension broke.

"I like you," said the unconcerned father. "So why are you really here?"

Vedran started to squirm. Stasia, drawing her arm against his windpipe, pressed on the dagger tip, piercing the fabric of his satin shirt and pricking his skin. He stilled.

Savik said nothing, simply watched Stasia with glittering eyes.

She answered him. "To sell you enough Semtex to blow up the Doge's Palace. I simply needed your son for the introduction."

The truth of the second statement rang in her words. It would convince the arms dealer that she really did have the powerful explosive.

"Indeed?" Savik tilted his head as if mildly curious. "I do not recall a need for Semtex."

"You will when you verify the quality of my product. Fortunately for you, I am in a bit of a hurry to offload it. There are certain *concerns* shall I say in Sicily who have tracked me to Venice. It would be better for me to sail without it. My loss will be your gain, *bello*."

Aco's eyes narrowed. He spat on the floor. "Let her gut the idiot, and be done with him. Then we can have some fun with her and her friend."

Olivia stepped in closer to Aco's side. "You would not like my idea of fun," she said in a dark whisper as she ran the gun's muzzle along his jaw.

A thrill of warning coursed down Stasia's spine at the sound of her new partner's voice. Prickles of sweat popped under her arms.

Clearly, Aco didn't feel the same dangerous edge. His face darkened.

Grazie a Dio Stasia wore a mask that hid most of her flushed features! Everything—including their lives—depended on how well she navigated the next few minutes with a roomful of deadly strangers.

Waving his hand, Savik shook his head. "There is no need for that, Aco. Unless *le belle signorine* have disrupted our celebration with a misleading sales pitch." He looked at Stasia. "You have the Semtex nearby?"

Stasia refrained from glancing toward Savik's remaining guard, who stood in the doorway to the entrance hall holding an HK416. He could take out all of them with an extended burst of the automatic rifle.

She needed to neutralize *that* threat first.

Her heartrate kicked up a notch as she nodded at Savik. "My men are waiting. They can bring it to me. But I think, *signore,* that this should be a private demonstration, if you take my meaning. Afterwards, we can toast our deal with Prosecco."

"A party for five, eh?" asked Savik, a gleam lighting his dark eyes. He studied her for a long moment before nodding at the guard armed with the HK. "Go."

Stasia addressed this guard in a confident, offhand manner. "The mahogany Serenella motorboat, the *Michelangelo*, thirty meters east. My men will likely be asleep. You have my permission to kick them awake, *signore*."

The guard, a darkly bearded bear of a man, flashed yellowing teeth at her before disappearing out the entrance to the palazzo.

Savik turned to the frozen partygoers, who'd watched the drama unfolding before them with varying degrees of fright and fascination. A few wore openly lascivious expressions, as if the promise of violence had whetted their libido. Given the likelihood that many of them were criminals mingling prior to a major arms sale, Stasia would love to see them in zip ties, but she couldn't afford to deal with them.

"My friends," said the Serb to his guests, "Party's over. I have business to conduct."

As Stasia watched them file out of the palazzo, she recalled Olivia's comment.

Trial by fire indeed.

TWELVE

Olivia watched as the murmuring masquerade guests shuffled through the archway into the palazzo's front hall. Next to her, Aco growled half a heartbeat before raising his hand to grapple with hers holding the appropriated Glock.

But Olivia's nerves had been strung tight ever since her new Italian friend had shocked the hell out of her with her explosive-and-unpredictable escalation. She'd been expecting the arms dealer's eldest son to make a move. As his arm came up, she gripped his wrist, twisting his arm and stepping behind him until he'd bent at the waist and his elbow faced upwards. Then she slammed the hand holding the 9mm into the exposed joint.

Aco screamed as the weighted strike fractured his elbow. At the same time, Olivia's thumb and forefinger pressed into the vulnerable points between the tendons at his wrist, preventing him from pulling free. She brought the muzzle to his throat.

"I wouldn't do that if I were you," she said to the man moaning and swaying at her feet, her hoarse whisper loud in the silent room.

When Savik would have helped Aco to his feet, Olivia stared at him. Whatever the Serb saw in her eyes made him halt.

Stasia, who'd orchestrated this play, intervened.

"Forgive my colleague's enthusiasm. We have had the misfortune not to be taken seriously at times by the men in our line of work. We have no patience for such nonsense." To emphasize her words, she squeezed Vedran's neck, causing him to choke and stagger.

Olivia, however, understood the underlying message: Stasia doubted Reardon's account about her.

After all of the Serb's guests had exited the palazzo, an oppressive tension thickened the air.

The guard that Olivia had knocked out began to stir. Olivia, letting go of Aco's wrist, hurried to kick the supine man under the chin, sending him to dreamland again. Then, backing away, she pointed the Glock at the injured Serb.

Savik, ignoring Aco's sweat-drenched face and Vedran's visible shaking, looked between Stasia and Olivia. "You realize that this Semtex of yours had better be the highest grade I have ever seen at the best price I have ever paid or I will gut both of you here as I sip the rest of my Prosecco."

He delivered this threat so smoothly and amiably that it took Olivia a second to realize what he'd said.

A shiver ran down her spine. The St. Michael medal heated on her bare collarbone.

Now she comprehended that "trial by fire" might be an especially apt metaphor. She had no idea where this operation was headed. What exactly would happen when the guard armed with the automatic rifle reached the motorboat?

Something the Italian team had already planned but Olivia hadn't been read in on.

She looked over at Stasia. "You have quite an interview technique."

Stasia grinned and shrugged.

Damn her, she enjoyed this.

Olivia wondered what the Italian's career must have been like for Stasia to engage in such high-octane tactics.

They didn't have to wait more than ten minutes before Savik's guard returned with two of Stasia's men at gunpoint carrying a large hard-sided storage case between them. Savik directed the two men to set the case on a glass-topped coffee table in the center of the room. As they did, he turned to the bearded guard and gestured.

"Your handgun," he said.

The guard pulled his holstered weapon and offered it to Savik grip first.

Then Savik shot the man on the floor in the head.

Olivia sucked in a shocked breath, her grip on the Glock wavering.

Savik looked over his shoulder at her before casually turning and gesturing with the gun. "The next one is for you, *dolcezza*, if you harm my son again."

Olivia restrained the urge to bare her teeth at him. No good would come of it. The room had turned into an emotional powder keg. The smallest spark would start a bloody inferno.

It was Stasia's turn to laugh.

Savik, eyes narrowed, aimed his gaze at the Italian spy.

"You think this amusing, *bella*?" asked the arms dealer in a silky voice. His hand holding the gun hadn't lowered.

"*Sì.*" Stasia nodded. "You are not at all worried about this one, are you, *amore mio*?" she asked, sliding the tip of her dagger up Vedran's side without taking her gaze from Savik. The timbre of her voice had taken on the same silky quality as his.

Olivia wondered if the other woman intentionally echoed the Serb.

Savik dismissed his younger son with a wave of his free hand. "He brought this upon himself when he let a woman do his thinking for him."

Olivia saw the younger man stiffen.

Was that Stasia's goal? To drive a wedge between father and son? Why?

A moment later, she understood the beauty of her Italian colleague's play.

Stasia nodded. "Very well, *signore*." She slipped off Vedran's back and stepped away from the terrified man. "Open the case, *tesoro mio*." She glanced toward Savik. "Would you care to see a demonstration of the Semtex?"

"What, here?" asked Savik, sounding a little horrified.

Stasia lifted a shoulder. "Why not? Vedran can prove his worth to you."

The arms dealer, his eldest son, and the bearded guard stood transfixed as Vedran, no longer trembling, approached the large container. The two Italian operatives had stepped away, their hands loose at their sides as they waited.

No one watched Olivia or Stasia for that matter.

Stasia's gaze landed on Olivia, who lifted her chin. Something was about to happen. She didn't know what, but Stasia had clearly gotten all of the pieces in place. If Olivia had been in Stasia's role, she would signal a waiting tac team....

The realization hit her like a load of bricks. She'd stumbled on an operation going hot.

Almost at the same instant, her ears caught the sound of the battering ram against the palazzo's massive front door. She began to slide toward the archway leading to the entrance hall.

"No, wait, Vedran!" said Savik, taking a step toward his younger son, who ignored him.

Olivia halted long enough to see Stasia throwing her knife at the bearded guard, who'd lifted his automatic rifle at his boss's shout. The guard crumpled, the knife handle sticking out of his upper back, bullets spraying an arc through the furniture and wall all the way to the high ceiling.

Then Savik, black fury transfiguring his Slavic features, lifted his weapon toward Stasia.

Olivia shot him even as Aco, his injured arm hanging at his side, rushed toward her.

He lunged the final meter as Olivia shifted to fire at him. As she squeezed the trigger, the enraged Serb knocked her arm up, sending the bullet into his shoulder instead of his torso and the Glock flying across the room. A moment later he loomed over her. His good hand found her throat.

Almost instantly his viselike grip cut off Olivia's air.

Her fingers scrabbled for purchase on his wrist. Her other hand searched for Beta's karambit where it hung in a thigh sheath under her gown. Darkness had begun to swamp her eyesight and clog her ears when Olivia managed to pull the skirt up and find the karambit's loop with her forefinger. She tugged the little Indonesian hawk-billed knife free.

Aco abruptly stiffened and jerked. His hold loosened enough for Olivia to drag in a mouthful of air. She sliced the karambit across his thigh even as she heard a pistol fire again and again.

Together, she and Aco tumbled to the floor, Olivia twisting in time for her upper body to land clear of the Serb, whose gasping breaths halted on a long exhale.

Stasia appeared holding a weapon. "*Mamma mia!*" she said, agitating the air around her with a hand. "*Per amor del Dio!* Why did you not just shoot the *bastardo*?"

Coughing, Olivia swallowed against the pain in her bruised throat. When she spoke, her words came out as a hoarse whisper. "I guess I didn't get the job, eh?"

After the Italian Special Forces breached the front door and the second team rappelled onto the roof, Stasia's team led Savik and Vedran in cuffs from the palazzo. The team medic removed Stasia's ARDA combat dagger from the bearded guard and returned it to her before they carried him out on a stretcher. The bodies of Aco and Savik's bodyguard they left for the time being on the floor of the salon, whose opulent furnishings had been destroyed, either by the uncontrolled burst from the HK416 or the melee that followed.

While Stasia dealt with the immediate aftermath of the raid, Olivia sat in a sumptuous carved Venetian chair painted gold with a green-velvet cushioned seat now heavily smeared with Aco's blood. The medic knelt at her side and checked her vitals, but the only thing really wrong with her was her swollen throat.

And maybe a bruised pelvis, but she'd suffered from that before. Larger, heavier men somehow always managed to land on her while sparring despite *Sensei* Mark drilling into her that she must at all costs avoid being brought down to the ground by a male opponent.

Pulling the jeweled half mask off, she sipped from the bottle of water the medic handed her and tugged the Mylar thermal blanket draped over her shoulders tighter. Then she toed off the ridiculous heels she wore. Her feet were killing her.

Stasia returned with the team leader of the tactical unit, a tall handsome man exuding no-nonsense strength and focus common among special forces the world over.

"Bring us some coffee and chocolate," she said to the medic as he stood.

Nodding, he turned to go.

Stasia glanced at Olivia's bare feet. "And find Ms. Markham some socks and boots, too," she said over her shoulder.

When she turned back, Olivia said, "You could have read me in on the raid. It almost went irredeemably pear-shaped."

Looking solemn, the Italian foreign intelligence officer nodded. "True, but then I would not have gotten as good a read on you, *cara*." As she said this, she handed Olivia the karambit.

"I see," said Olivia, accepting the small knife with its hooked tip caked with dried blood. She wondered what Stasia had learned about her.

The other woman didn't elaborate, however. Instead, she said, "Major Antonelli has brought me some news. Would you care to accompany us?"

That set Olivia's antennae buzzing.

They waited until the medic returned with a pair of small men's combat boots and thick wool socks. Once Olivia had donned her new, less elegant, footwear, Major Antonelli led them to the massive carved wooden door, which now leaned against the wall to the side of the doorway into the office. To Olivia's amusement, she realized that the Italian Special Forces team had removed the door hinges rather than use a shaped charge.

Inside the office, two commandoes went through the paper files while a third sat at the heavy Rococo wooden desk whose burnished surface disappeared under a mess of filled ashtrays, empty vodka bottles, and loose ammunition.

Major Antonelli walked to the side of the tech specialist at the desktop computer. Stasia and Olivia followed.

"Lieutenant, show us the files you found."

The lieutenant walked them through a cache of files on Savik's hard drive. It was clear from the documents and images that the Serb arms dealer had already sold his prize offering: a weaponized MQ-1C Unmanned Aerial Vehicle also known as a Gray Eagle.

"A Predator drone with Hellfire missiles," said Olivia.

Stasia studied Olivia. "You are not surprised."

Olivia shook her head. "I received some unverified intel about Savik setting up an auction. That's why I contacted you."

Major Antonelli, who'd been silent during the presentation, spoke now. "The 38th Wing of our Air Force used this particular Gray Eagle for surveillance until early this year when its sensors failed, and it was pulled from service. We only just discovered that it had been stolen last week."

Olivia looked between the two Italians. "Your country hasn't yet notified mine about the missing drone."

Stasia shook her head. "We are still working to repair our relationship with the United States. We did not want to alert the CIA if we could recover the Gray Eagle ourselves."

Olivia nodded. AISE had been formed in 2007 from the disgraced former Italian-military-intelligence agency that had given the U.S. government forged documents showing Saddam Hussein purchasing so-called 'yellowcake' uranium from Niger. It had been a major factor in the U.S. going to war with Iraq.

Olivia had a decision to make: alert the CIA, thereby justifying going off the reservation after the fact or keep the revelation to herself to build a bridge with the Italians.

She looked from Stasia to Major Antonelli. "I see no reason to alert Reardon," she said slowly. "But I will need to get copies of all the information on Savik's buyers you recover. My intel links him with a terrorist connected to the Berlin Christmas market bombing and the suicide bombers in Brussels."

Stasia relaxed a fraction. If she hadn't been watching, Olivia might have missed the micromovement. Major Antonelli gave her a curt nod.

A commando came into the office just then.

"Sir, we found something you should see."

Major Antonelli turned to go.

Time to see how far this budding relationship had developed.

Olivia stepped forward. "I want to come along."

The tac team leader turned slightly. He glanced at Stasia, whose nearly imperceptible nod told Olivia what she needed to know.

The three of them followed the commando through several rooms, including the salon. As they walked through, Olivia noticed that the two dead Serbs had been removed. She wondered idly how long it would take for AISE cleaners to arrive and begin the process of repairing damage and replacing destroyed furnishings. Given that AISE, like the CIA, was forbidden by law to operate domestically, she'd wager before the tac team left, and the cleanup would be museum quality.

The commando led them to the stairs in the entrance hall where the ornate railing hung from the gold-veined-ivory marble steps, which had been deeply gouged from dozens of rounds. Vivid red spatters on the brocaded wallpaper next to the stairs hung over a meter-wide pool of blood where the Serbian guard had stood. Someone had wiped the steps, smearing the blood in the process but making them less treacherous.

Once upstairs, the soldier led them into a suite whose double doors stood wide at the end of a short hallway.

Inside, they were greeted with the image of a dormitory filled with cheap iron beds and thin, bare mattresses that were dirty and stained. Half a dozen young women in various stages of dress sat staring mutely at them. One lay motionless on her cot, bruises and burns mottling her arms, throat, and legs. Deep reddish brown stained her gown at the apex of her thighs. By the looks of it, she'd been dead for some time.

Animals.

Olivia felt more than saw Stasia stiffen next to her.

"*Animali,*" said Stasia under her breath, echoing Olivia's thoughts.

Olivia placed her hand on the other woman's arm. A tremor convulsed under her fingers. Stasia's clenched jaw revealed her struggle to contain her reaction.

As for Olivia, her stomach roiled, but there was no way that she would give in to her anguish and nausea in front of the suffering women.

"What do you want to do about them, sir?" asked the young commando.

"Contact the local authorities after we are through here—" began Major Antonelli.

"To begin, you can get them out of this room," said Stasia, cutting him off. The venom in her previously mellifluous voice stunned Olivia. "Have your medic look at all of them to make sure none has any urgent medical needs. And bring them food and water for the love of God!"

The commando stood impassive under Stasia's tongue lashing. When she'd finished, his gaze flicked to his commanding officer, who dipped his chin.

Five minutes later, four commandoes arrived with stretchers and carried two of the women from the room. The other four women managed to hobble out of the suite with support from two more commandoes. Major Antonelli waited until his men had disappeared before looking around the room once and then excusing himself to oversee his team's departure. It was now four a.m., and dawn already lightened the sky. The tac team needed to be gone from the palazzo before sunrise when the risk of them being spotted increased exponentially.

When they were alone, Stasia walked over to the bed with the body of the young woman, sinking to her knees next to it. She stared at the woman's pale features.

"I knew Savik trafficked women," she said after several long moments. "But I did not fully understand what that means. Perhaps if I had, I would have worked harder to raid the palazzo before she died." Stasia's harsh voice condemned herself.

Olivia came to stand next to the AISE officer. "Leave blame where it belongs: with predators like Savik and his customers."

Stasia said nothing, simply crossed her arms and scoffed.

God, Olivia was tired. Had it really only been twenty-four hours since she'd been in Katowice with Beta, rescuing other women from sex slavery? She stifled a yawn then heard voices downstairs as the cleaners arrived.

"The women shouldn't be here to witness the cleanup," said Olivia. "They should be at the hospital."

She looked over at Stasia, whose faraway gaze suggested that her thoughts had been anywhere but on the remnants of the operation.

Stasia blinked and stirred. She returned Olivia's look. In that moment, something passed between them. The St. Michael medal on Olivia's chest warmed in a ray of morning light coming through a slit in the heavy drapes on the tall windows behind them. She touched a fingertip to it.

"Can you afford to delay your return to Prague?" asked Stasia, concern heavy on her features, now illuminated by sunlight. There was a world of meaning in that simple question.

Looking down at the dead woman's frozen features, Olivia found that she didn't care.

"Can we use the *Michelangelo*?" she asked instead.

Stasia's gaze searched Olivia's before at last a tentative smile softened her expression. "But of course, *cara*."

"Good."

"I will go tell Major Antonelli that we will need some help with the women on stretchers."

"And her." Olivia lifted her chin to indicate the dead woman. "I'll wait with her."

Stasia blinked several times before nodding and turning sharply on her heel.

Apropos of nothing, Olivia noticed that Stasia had also donned military boots as the Italian strode out of the suite. She almost laughed, but an edge of something like panic or hysteria warned her that she was dangerously close to losing it.

Instead, she closed her eyes for a moment to gather her composure. *God, give me strength.*

Sighing, she opened her eyes again. That's when her gaze caught on something white under the dead woman's shoulders.

An almost painful surge of adrenaline coursed through her as she leaned forward to tug the material free.

It was an embroidered *taqiyah* just like the one that Mr. X had worn that night in Berlin.

Olivia crumpled the skullcap in her fist.

It didn't matter. She knew what she had to do. She had to make sure Savik's victims found safe haven. She had to make sure that *they* mattered.

And the first step was putting them first. Ranking them higher than that terrorist bastard.

Stasia came up behind her a few minutes later. Two commandos followed with a stretcher and gently lifted the young woman's body onto it. They watched in silence as the two soldiers left.

Then Stasia held out the mask that Olivia had abandoned. In her other hand, she carried the mask that she herself had worn during the evening.

"You Americans love your superheroes, do you not?" At Olivia's bemused nod, she continued, "Perhaps we can borrow their habit of going incognito. It will be daylight when we bring the women to the hospital."

Olivia took the mask and studied it more closely. It was an asymmetrical satin half mask in royal blue and silver. Wispy blue-and-silver feathers affixed to the temple by a jewel-encrusted brooch and blue ribbon added weight. A familiar diamond pattern decorated the forehead.

In the corner of one eye, an embroidered silver tear slid onto the cheek next to the nose.

"Seems appropriate," she said in response to Stasia's suggestion as she traced that glittering frozen tear.

She tied the mask on and looked up at the other woman, who had likewise donned her mask.

"Let's go."

ABOUT LIANE ZANE

Liane Zane is the cover identity of a novelist who is an expert at hiding in plain sight. She has spent time interrogating a former Army intelligence officer and engaging in Open-Source Intelligence (OSINT) activities related to Italian slang words for naughty body parts and the proclivities of Eastern European criminals. She spends her days drinking New England chocolate-raspberry coffee and gazing at the magical brook in her back yard as she plots her romantic thrillers or walking her dogs along mountain trails near her estate-like home.

THE HARLEQUIN PROTOCOL (Book Two) is the second book in Liane's series, THE UNSANCTIONED GUARDIANS, which narrates the genesis of the Wild *Elioud* (Olivia, Beta, and Stasia) first introduced in THE *ELIOUD* LEGACY into a disciplined team of covert advocates for innocent victims, especially of sex trafficking and assault. THE COVERT GUARDIAN (Book One) and THE GUARDIAN INITIATIVE (Book Three) complete the prequel trilogy.

THE *ELIOUD* LEGACY comprises THE HARLEQUIN & THE DRANGÙE (Olivia & Mihàil's story), THE FLOWER & THE BLACKBIRD (Stasia & Miró's story), and THE DRAKA & THE GIANT (Beta and András's story). All three books tell the complex legacy of the *Elioud* descendants of the Fallen Watcher Angels and are therefore best read in order.

Visit www.lianezane.com for updates and to buy merchandise related to the series.

9 781963 515022